MEET THE GIRLS FROM CABIN SIX

KATIE, a born leader, is going to make sure her summer at Camp Sunnyside isn't ruined by a bunch of boys!

MEGAN has her head in the clouds most of the time, but she'll do her part to keep the enemy out.

SARAH will be happy at Camp Sunnyside as long as she can sit and read . . . and nobody forces her to participate in camp activities.

TRINA, sensitive and caring as always, just wants everyone to be happy . . . and this year that's almost impossible.

ERIN thinks she's outgrown camp and would rather be hanging around the country-club pool flirting with the boys . . . instead of playing silly camp games with the girls.

Look for More Fun and Games with
CAMP SUNNYSIDE FRIENDS
by Marilyn Kaye
from Avon Camelot

(#2) CABIN SIX PLAYS CUPID

Coming Soon

(#3) COLOR WAR

MARILYN KAYE is the author of many popular books for young readers, including the "Out of This World" series and the "Sisters" books. She is an associate professor at St. John's University and lives in Brooklyn, New York.

Camp Sunnyside is the camp Marilyn Kaye wishes that she had gone to every summer when she was a kid.

No Boys Allowed!

Marilyn Kaye

AN AVON CAMELOT BOOK

CAMP SUNNYSIDE FRIENDS #1: NO BOYS ALLOWED! is an original publication of Avon Books. This work has never before appeared in book form.

AVON BOOKS
A division of
The Hearst Corporation
105 Madison Avenue
New York, New York 10016

First Avon Camelot Printing: June 1989

CAMELOT TRADEMARK REG. U.S. PAT. OFF. AND IN OTHER COUNTRIES, MARCA REGISTRADA, HECHO EN U.S.A.

Printed in the U.S.A.

OPM 10 9 8 7 6 5 4 3 2

For Sam Blasco

Chapter 1

Katie Dillon picked up a brand-new tee shirt, folded it carefully, and placed it in the open suitcase lying on her bed. Then she took it out, unfolded it, and for the zillionth time that day admired the design on the front. It was a big yellow sun with rays shooting out from it. And underneath the sun, in bright orange letters, were the words "Camp Sunnyside." A tingle of anticipation ran through her. Tomorrow, at this time, she'd be wearing this shirt.

Suddenly, she couldn't wait. She slipped it on over the plain tee shirt she was already wearing.

"Katie! Could you come down here?" Her mother's voice floated up to her room. Katie skipped out of the room and ran downstairs to the kitchen.

Her mother was sewing at the kitchen table, where more tee shirts and a pile of freshly ironed shorts were stacked. One pair sat on her lap, and Mrs. Dillon took a couple of quick stitches before looking up.

"Katie, why are you wearing that now? You'll get it dirty."

"I just wanted to get in the mood," Katie replied, joining her mother at the table.

Her mother laughed. "You've been in the mood for a month now! I don't think you've talked about anything else but going off to camp." The look she gave her daughter was almost sad. "I must say, you're awfully eager to leave home. Don't you get the least bit homesick when you're away at camp?"

"Oh, I'll miss you and Dad," Katie assured her. Just then, the back door swung open, and her two older brothers charged in. As usual they didn't bother with greetings. They both headed directly for the refrigerator.

"But I won't miss them," Katie added darkly. It would have been bad enough having one brother two years older, she thought. Having *twin* brothers was impossible.

"The same goes for us," Michael replied, making a face at her. Katie stuck out her tongue in response.

"Boys, Katie," Mrs. Dillon murmured automatically. "No fighting tonight, okay? It's Katie's last evening at home, and we won't have her with us again for eight weeks."

Katie knew what was coming, and the twins didn't disappoint her. They both cheered. Mrs. Dillon frowned at them, but Katie wasn't bothered at all. She was just as happy to be getting away from them.

Her mother bit off her thread. "All done." She added the shorts to the pile. Katie leaned over and examined the shorts, all neatly labeled "K. Dillon."

"Thanks, Mom."

Her mother sighed. "I remember the first time I did this for you."

"Three years ago," Katie said promptly. "I was eight when I first went to Sunnyside."

"You were just a baby."

"And were you ever scared!" This came from Peter, who had settled himself at the table with a bowl of ice cream.

"Yeah," added Michael, joining him. "You cried all night."

Katie glared at them. *She* didn't remember crying. Okay, maybe she'd whimpered a little. "That's because I didn't know what to expect," she said with dignity. "Now I know exactly what it's going to be like."

She pulled her bare feet up on the chair and wrapped her arms around her knees. "It's going to be exactly the same group," she said dreamily, "in the same cabin, with the same counselor—"

"Sounds boring to me," Peter interjected.

"Are you kidding?" Boring was the last word she'd use to describe Camp Sunnyside. "We've got horses, and a lake where we go canoeing, and a swimming pool, and tennis courts, and—"

Michael whistled. "Hey, wait a minute. This doesn't sound so bad. Maybe *we* should be going to Sunnyside."

3

Katie knew he was joking, but she played along. "You can't," she said smugly. "Because that's the best thing about Sunnyside. No boys!"

Peter reached over and took one of the tee shirts from the pile. Then he got up and held it in front of his chest. "I'm a Sunnyside girl," he sang in a high squeaky voice, "with a Sunnyside smile . . ."

Katie leaped up, ran around the table, and grabbed the tee shirt away. She could only take so much teasing. Hearing her creepy brother mock the official camp song was more than she could bear.

"Kids! Cool it!" Mrs. Dillon pleaded. "Your father's going to be home any minute. Could we *please* have some peace and quiet and a nice family dinner? Katie, take this stuff upstairs and finish packing."

Katie grabbed her shorts and shirts, shot one last ferocious glare at her brothers, and ran out. Back in her room, she piled the shorts and tee shirts in the suitcase, and added socks, underwear, and tennis shoes. She decided she'd better take the tee shirt off before dinner, so it would be clean enough to wear tomorrow. But before she did, she took one last look in the mirror.

Had she changed much since last year? Stuck in the frame of the mirror was a snapshot, and Katie pulled it out. There they were, the girls of cabin six. Katie examined herself, sitting cross-legged on the ground in front. Then she looked back at her reflection.

No, she'd hardly changed at all. She was two

4

inches taller, and maybe a little thinner, but still average for her age. Maybe her straight, medium brown hair was a little longer, but it didn't look that different. She turned to the side and checked out her profile. No chest yet, but that was okay. She just hoped all the others weren't ahead of her in that area.

She smiled as she looked at the other girls in the photograph. After three years together, they were like a family. No, she decided, better than a family. They didn't fight and tease and get on each other's nerves. Well, not that much.

It was funny, she thought, how they never got together during the school year. They didn't live that far apart. They'd figured it out once, and realized that no one lived more than three hours from anyone else. At the end of every summer, when they separated, they talked about getting together during the school year. But they never did.

She examined the individual faces in the picture. There was Trina, her best summer friend, standing straight and tall, with her tee shirt neatly tucked in her shorts. This picture had been taken on the last day of camp, but Trina's uniform was still unbelievably clean and crisp. It was typical of her, Katie thought. Trina was the sensible type, and never got as rowdy as the rest of them.

Tiny Megan, with her unruly red curls hanging in her eyes, looked spaced out, as usual. Megan was always daydreaming. Chubby Sarah's wire-rimmed glasses were perched on the tip of her

5

nose. Her expression was intense and serious. Erin was the only one who really looked like she was posing. She had her hands on her hips, and her smile looked just a little fake.

The Sunnyside girls, the cabin six gang . . . tomorrow they'd all be together again. Right this very minute, they were probably packing, just like Katie. And as Katie gazed at the snapshot, she wondered if they were all feeling just as excited.

Trina Sandburg checked the contents of her suitcase one last time, and nodded in satisfaction. Every item she needed was there, neatly folded and tucked away, and everything was in its proper place. She'd planned her packing carefully, so she could make best use of the space and nothing would get wrinkled.

She had just closed the suitcase and snapped the locks when her mother bounced into the room. "Trina, darling, want to go shopping tomorrow? There's a great sale at the mall."

Trina smiled and shook her head. "I'm going to camp tomorrow, Mom, remember?"

Her mother slapped her own forehead. "Oh my goodness, that's right! Tomorrow's Sunday!" She shook her head ruefully. "It's a good thing you're so organized, Trina."

Trina laughed. "One of us has to be." She gazed fondly at her scatterbrained mother. She'd always been that way, and ever since the divorce five months ago, she'd become even more so. As an only child, Trina sometimes felt like *she* was the mother. Often, she had to remind her mother that they needed groceries, that the rent on their apartment was due, that one of them had an appointment with the dentist.

She didn't mind, though. In fact, Trina liked being in charge. And despite the fact that her mother could be a little dippy, she was the warmest, kindest, most loving person in the world.

Her mother demonstrated this right that minute, throwing her arms around Trina and hugging her tightly. "I'm going to miss you, darling. What am I going to do without you?"

Her words revived some worries Trina had been trying not to think about. "Are you going to be okay, Mom?"

Her mother released her, and held her at arm's length. "Absolutely. And it's going to be very good for me to be alone." Her voice rang with confidence. "I've been relying on you much too much since your father and I divorced, and you've had to take on too many responsibilities. It's time for you to enjoy being a child again. Let loose! Be a wild, silly kid!"

"Okay, Mom." Then she sniffed. "Do I smell something burning?"

Her mother clasped her hand over her mouth. "Oh no! I forgot about the pizza!" Together, they raced down the hall to the kitchen.

Later that evening, after they'd eaten the slightly blackened pizza, Trina thought about

7

what her mother had said about being a kid again. What her mother didn't realize was that Trina *liked* taking care of people. Even at camp, she often found herself acting like a parent to the other kids in her cabin. They could all get so crazy sometimes. Trina was always trying to talk Katie and the others out of one wild scheme or another.

But sometimes Trina did wish she could just let loose and act crazy too. People always told her she was unusually responsible and sensible. Well, maybe she was too much that way. Maybe, this summer, *she'd* get involved with a wild scheme or two.

Because if there was ever a place where a person could get wild and crazy, it was definitely Sunnyside.

"Megan?"

Megan Lindsay gazed vaguely at her father standing in her doorway. "Yeah, Dad?"

"Why don't you give me your suitcase now and I'll put it in the trunk of the car."

Megan looked at the empty duffel bag lying on the floor. "Uh, I haven't exactly finished packing yet."

Her father came into her room and peered into the bag. "Megan!" he exclaimed. "You haven't even started yet!"

Megan was contrite. "Sorry, Dad. I guess I was daydreaming."

Her father shook his head wearily. "Tell me something new."

Megan hopped up off her bed. "I'm going to do it right this minute. It'll only take five minutes, I promise."

And that's all it took. Five minutes later, Megan was struggling to zip the duffel bag.

Her mother appeared at the door. "How's it going?"

"I'm all ready," Megan told her proudly. "Could you help me close this zipper?"

"Good heavens," Mrs. Lindsay murmured as she peered inside the bag. "Didn't you fold anything?"

Megan shook her head. It was much quicker just to cram everything in. And what was the point of folding the stuff? She was just going to be unpacking it all tomorrow. How wrinkled could things get in one day?

"Are you sure you remembered everything?" her mother asked. "Shirts, shorts, bathing suit, sneakers, pajamas—"

"Everything," Megan replied. "It's all there."

"Underwear?"

Megan looked at her blankly. Then an abashed grin spread across her face. "Well, maybe not everything."

"Oh, Megan," her mother sighed. "How do you manage without me at Sunnyside? Or maybe, at Sunnyside, you don't have your head in the clouds the way you do at home."

Megan looked thoughtful. "I'm not sure. But I

guess I'm about the same at Sunnyside as I am here."

Mrs. Lindsay laughed as she rearranged the items in the duffel bag and added the underwear. "Then heaven help your counselor, that's all I can say."

Counselor ... Megan wondered if they'd have Nina again, like last year. Nina was okay, but it would be nice to have someone new. Maybe she'd be someone mysterious ... an heiress, running away from her palatial mansion where her hard-hearted father had kept her imprisoned for decades. No, wait, not a father, a boyfriend, that was much more romantic. And maybe he'd come to Sunnyside, looking for her, and she'd confide in Megan, and Megan would hide her, and then she'd confront the boyfriend, and he'd be *so* handsome and—

"Megan!"

"Huh?"

"Would you like to come down off your cloud long enough to join us for dinner?"

Megan didn't mind shoving her fantasy aside for the moment. After all, tomorrow she would be at camp. And if ever there was a place where a fantasy just might come true, it was Sunnyside.

Sarah Fine lowered the top of her suitcase as far as it would go. Then she sat on it.

It still wouldn't close. She tried standing on it. Then she tried jumping.

"Alison!" she shrieked. From across the hall, her older sister yelled back, "What do you want?"

"Help!"

When Alison walked in, she started laughing. "What are you doing?"

"What does it look like I'm doing?" Sarah growled. "I'm trying to close this suitcase." She stopped her useless pounding. "You're always bragging about your muscles and how strong you are. Prove it!"

Alison stared at the suitcase. "No way. Mister Universe couldn't close that suitcase. What have you got in there anyway?"

"Camp stuff," Sarah said vaguely, hoping Alison wouldn't decide to investigate. Her hopes were in vain. Alison pushed past her and opened the suitcase.

"Oh, Sarah," she murmured sadly.

From the tone of her voice, it could have been bottles of whiskey and cartons of cigarettes. "It's just a few books," Sarah said.

"A few! You must have twenty, thirty books in here! Is that all you plan to do at camp? *Read?*"

"You make it sound illegal!" Sarah exclaimed. "I like to read. Is that a crime?"

"Camp isn't for reading," Alison argued. "It's for swimming, and riding horses, and getting outdoor exercise! You could definitely *use* a little exercise," she added, looking pointedly at Sarah's protruding stomach.

"Yuck," was Sarah's only response.

"I don't understand why you go to camp anyway, if you don't like the activities. Dad wouldn't make you go if you didn't want to."

She was right, Sarah thought. Their father was an absolute pushover when it came to his daughters. Ever since their mother had died, when they were very young, he'd pretty much given them anything they wanted. Luckily for him, they didn't take advantage of this.

But Sarah didn't want to get out of going to camp. "I like Sunnyside," Sarah replied. "I mean, I like the people. I've got friends there."

"Well, I wish your friends would make you get involved," Alison stated. She made a halfhearted attempt to close the suitcase. "Forget it. You absolutely can't fit all these books in here."

Sarah looked at the suitcase in dismay. How could she go to Sunnyside without enough reading material for the summer? Sunnyside might have pools and tennis courts, but it didn't have a bookstore or a library.

Her expression must have been particularly woebegone, because a flash of sympathy crossed Alison's face. "Look, how about if I lend you my backpack? You can cram your books in there."

Sarah grinned. "Thanks, Al."

"But promise me one thing," Alison continued. "You'll do something at Sunnyside this summer besides read."

"I promise," Sarah said solemnly. And she knew she would. She'd be doing a lot of creative thinking, dreaming up the excuses that would get her out of doing *everything*.

Erin Chapman stamped her foot on the floor, even though she knew it wouldn't do any good. "But I don't want to go to camp!"

"I don't understand what's gotten into you, Erin," her mother said. She wiped a nonexistent speck of dust from the leather suitcase. "You've always loved going to Sunnyside in the past."

"I'm too *old* for camp," Erin argued.

"That's ridiculous," her mother said calmly. "Sunnyside goes through age thirteen. And you told me yourself that all your cabin friends are going back this year. Don't you want to be with your friends?"

Erin sat down on her bed, and gazed up at the lace hanging from the canopy. She couldn't think of a snappy response to that question.

Sure, she wanted to be with her camp friends. But the thought of spending the summer at an all-girls camp, wearing those stupid shorts and tee shirts and playing volleyball, while all her friends here in town were hanging out at the country club pool wearing bikinis and flirting with the teenage boys—it just wasn't fair!

"Tell me," her mother said, sitting on the bed next to her. "Tell me the real reason you don't want to go to camp this summer."

Erin had a pretty strong suspicion her mother wouldn't exactly approve of her motives. "Well," she said slowly, "I might get homesick for you and Daddy."

"Really?" Mrs. Chapman looked surprised. "You've never gotten homesick before."

"There's always a first time." She turned pleading eyes to her mother. "Can't I stay home? Please?"

"But your father and I are going to Europe, like we do every summer. And I've given the housekeeper the time off. You can't stay here alone."

"I could stay with Marcia," Erin offered eagerly. *That* would be perfect. Her best friend's parents wouldn't pay any attention to them. They could have parties every night.

Her mother raised her eyebrows and the corner of her mouth twitched. "And why would you be any less homesick for Daddy and me at Marcia's than you'd be at camp?"

She had her there. Erin fell back on the bed and let out a long, mournful sigh.

"Cheer up," Mrs. Chapman said briskly. "You'll have a wonderful time. You always do."

Well, it would be fun hanging out with the cabin six gang. But a whole summer with no boys . . .

"Would you like to take my pearl necklace?" her mother offered.

Erin brightened slightly, and nodded. She was always trying to get her mother to let her wear that necklace. It would definitely impress the others.

But as her mother left the room to get the necklace, her smile faded. Where would she wear the pearl necklace anyway? Around the camp fire? At movie-on-the-lake night? There was never any point in dressing up at Sunnyside, Erin thought miserably. Not when there weren't any boys to dress up for.

Katie was just getting into bed when her bedroom door burst open.

"Don't you ever knock?" she demanded of Michael and Peter.

"We just wanted to say good-bye," Michael said. "We've got baseball practice early tomorrow, so we might be gone before you're up."

"And we've got a little going-away present for you," Peter added.

Katie stiffened. What was it this time? A live frog? A can of worms?

The wooden box they handed her had a fancy design engraved on the top. It was actually pretty. Katie opened it slowly, prepared for something disgusting to jump out.

But the inside was empty, lined in velvet, and divided into compartments.

"We made it in that crafts class we were taking," Michael told her. "We figured you could use it for souvenirs or something."

Katie grinned. "Gee, thanks."

Peter scratched his head and studied his sneakers. "Uh, look, kid, we'll miss you. Sort of."

Katie nodded. "Yeah. I guess I'll kind of miss you too. Sort of."

The boys left, and Katie lay back on her pillow. Her twin brothers might be obnoxious and stupid, but sometimes they were okay. Maybe she *would* miss them. But that didn't mean she couldn't be perfectly happy without them for eight weeks.

And as she closed her eyes, her head filled with visions of camp fires and horses and swimming, canoe races and cookouts, pillow fights and nature walks.

And no boys.

Chapter 2

Katie leaned across the sleeping woman sitting next to her on the bus and looked out the window. She saw the same green, rolling countryside she'd been seeing for the past two hours. Pretty, but not too thrilling.

She sank back into her seat. This was the first year she'd been allowed to travel to Sunnyside on her own. Every other year her parents had driven her, but this year she'd begged to go alone on the bus.

And even though the ride was kind of boring, she was glad she'd gotten her good-byes over with at home. All that hugging and kissing at camp could get a little messy. She was always on the verge of crying when her parents left, and that put a damper on her first day at camp.

She leaned over again to look out the window. And then she saw it—the exit sign to Pine Ridge. She would have shrieked except for the lady sleeping next to her. She had arrived!

The bus pulled into the little bus station, which really wasn't a bus station at all, just a convenience store with a bench in front and a sign that read BUS STOP. Katie jumped up, pulled her suitcase down from the overhead rack, and was waiting by the door as the bus came to a halt.

In the parking lot, she spotted one of the familiar minivans, with the beaming sun and CAMP SUNNYSIDE painted on the side. A lanky, brown-haired boy, a man really, wearing a Sunnyside tee shirt, leaned against it.

He waved when he saw Katie. "You headed for Sunnyside?" he called out to her. When Katie nodded, he grabbed her suitcase. "I'm Teddy Hughes, the new camp driver and handyman. We have to wait for one more bus. It's due any minute."

"Okay," Katie said, and tried not to let him see that she was looking him over. He was cuter than last year's handyman, she decided.

Teddy grinned easily at her. "This your first year at Sunnyside?"

"Oh no," Katie replied quickly. "I've been coming here for ages." Teddy smiled, nodded, and then there was silence. Katie tried to think of a way to make conversation. "Do you think you'll like being at a girls' camp?"

"Sure," Teddy said easily. "I like girls. Here comes the other bus." He headed toward it as the bus came to a stop and the doors opened.

Katie decided to get into the van, so she could

grab a window seat. As she was climbing in, she heard a familiar voice behind her.

"Katie, hi."

Katie whirled around. "Trina!" she shrieked. The girls threw their arms around each other. Then Katie started jumping up and down. Trina didn't, but that wasn't her style. Katie could tell Trina was just as happy to see her as she was to see Trina.

"You look wonderful," Trina said.

"You do too," Katie bubbled. She was very glad to see Trina hadn't changed anymore than Katie had. She was a little taller, and her dark hair was cut shorter, but she wasn't showing any major signs of maturity.

Three younger campers brushed past them and climbed into the van. Trina and Katie followed them, talking nonstop.

"It's so great being back," Katie declared as the van started off. "I can't wait to see the whole gang."

"Me too," Trina said. "Have you got any schemes cooked up for us yet?"

Katie laughed. "Not yet, but I'm sure I'll think of something. And you'd better go along with whatever it is!"

"Absolutely," Trina assured her. "As long as it's not going to get us sent home."

Since they were upper-grade campers, they ignored the three younger ones in the van. That didn't seem to bother the younger girls, though.

They'd been giggling nonstop since the van started moving.

"We're lucky we have Nina for a counselor," Katie mused. "She lets us get away with lots more than other counselors."

Trina shook her head. "But we're not going to have Nina. She's not coming back to Sunnyside this year."

Katie was surprised. "How do you know?"

Trina reached into her pocket and pulled out a postcard. "I got this from her." She handed it to Katie.

The message was brief.

Dear Trina, Remember my talking about Mike, my boyfriend? Well, we've decided to get married! So I won't be back this summer. Please share my news with all the girls in cabin six. I'll miss you all, but have a wonderful summer. Love, Nina.

Katie felt a twinge of disappointment. Nina had been a great counselor, very easygoing, and she pretty much let the girls do anything they wanted.

"Darn," Katie muttered. "I wanted everything to be the same. I wonder who they're going to stick us with?"

"I'm sure the new counselor will be okay," Trina said. "We have to give her a chance."

Typical Trina, Katie thought, always trying to be fair. Oh well, a new counselor wouldn't be a major change. She looked at the postcard again. "Married. Yuck."

Trina nodded. "It's definitely not what it's cracked up to be." Her tone was suddenly sad, and Katie looked at her curiously.

"My parents got divorced this year," Trina told her.

"Oh, Trina!" Katie gazed at her in dismay. Trina just smiled slightly and shrugged.

"It's okay. They were fighting all the time, and I'm kind of glad they split up. I still see my dad on weekends. And both Mom and Dad seem a lot happier now."

"That's good," Katie said uncertainly. She couldn't imagine her own parents splitting up. On the other hand, it was too bad she couldn't get divorced from her brothers. . . .

She wondered how Trina was *really* feeling. She wasn't the type to spill her guts about everything the way Katie did. She's probably sadder than she's acting, Katie decided. And she made a vow to watch out for Trina that summer, to get her involved with something really wild so she wouldn't think about her parents. She tried to think of possible schemes—a friendly rivalry with another cabin, maybe? Some tricks they could play on the new counselor?

Her thoughts were interrupted by a shrill chorus of screams from the younger campers. "Look!" Trina exclaimed.

They were passing under the archway that announced they were entering Camp Sunnyside. Katie's heart leaped. The three little kids were now bouncing up and down on their seats. Katie felt like doing that too, but she figured she had to preserve a bit of upper-grade dignity. So she contented herself with grabbing Trina's hand and squeezing it.

Sunnyside! The place looked wonderful. They spent the next few minutes happily identifying each landmark.

"There's the arts and crafts cabin!" Katie announced.

"Look, the activity hall got painted," Trina pointed out.

"Ooh! There's Darrell!" The girls waved frantically at the handsome, tanned swimming coach. When he waved back, they put their hands over their hearts and pretended to swoon. The cabin six girls always did that when Darrell's name was mentioned.

In the distance, Katie spotted the stables and the lake and the cabins. All over the place, there were girls lugging suitcases and knapsacks. The van finally came to a halt in front of the main building. Campers and parents were milling around a long table and forming lines in front of signs labeled A—E, F—J, and so on.

And in the middle of it all stood Ms. Winkle, flustered and harried as usual. The camp director looked like she was trying to do a million things at once—answer questions, give directions, and greet campers. Katie hugged herself in happiness. Except for Nina, everything at Sunnyside was exactly the same.

"All out for Sunnyside!" Teddy declared. It was a totally unnecessary announcement. The girls were already piling out of the van. Katie and Trina separated to go to their lines.

Standing in line, Katie had a momentary pang of worry. What if Ms. Winkle had decided to split up cabin six? After that business last summer, when they'd short sheeted all the beds in cabin five, she'd threatened to.

"Katie Dillon," she told the counselor at the table. The girl checked her list and said, "Cabin six." Katie breathed a temporary sigh of relief. It couldn't be permanent until she knew the whole gang would be there.

Trina ran over to her. "Did you get six?" When Katie nodded, she grinned. "C'mon, let's go see if the others are there."

They stopped to say hello to Ms. Winkle who, as usual, called Katie, Trina and Trina, Katie. But she seemed glad to see them anyway.

"I guess she forgot about last summer," Trina told Katie as they started up the slope toward their cabin.

Katie's eyes twinkled mischievously. "Well, we'll have to come up with something this year to make us totally unforgettable." She laughed at Trina's expression of alarm. "Oh, come on Trina,

I would never come up with anything that could get us in *real* trouble."

"I don't know about that," Trina murmured. "Remember that time we—" She didn't get to finish. Two figures had emerged from cabin six and were now running toward them.

"Sarah! Megan!" Katie ran forward with Trina close behind. And for the next few minutes, the four girls screamed and hugged and bounced up and down. With their arms around each other, they made their way into the cabin.

Good old cabin six. It looked just like it did on the first day last year, and the year before, and the year before that. There were the two sets of bunk beds, and the one single bed. Sarah and Megan had already claimed the same bunk beds they had every year, and Trina and Katie took the other set, as usual. Erin always had the separate single bed. She said being on top would make her airsick, and having someone over her would make her feel trapped.

The whitewashed walls were bare, but that didn't last long. As the girls chattered and caught up with one another, they pulled posters and pictures from their suitcases and began tacking them up.

"Have you seen the new counselor?" Katie asked Sarah and Megan.

"Not yet," Sarah said. "She's probably one of the girls down at the registration table." She bit her lower lip. "I hope she's not one of those gung ho types."

Katie nodded knowingly. They all knew how Sarah tried to get out of doing outdoor things. And Nina had never bugged her much about it.

Megan was poking around curiously in Sarah's suitcase. Then she squealed and pulled out a box. "Sarah! You got it!" When she held up the box so the others could read the label, Trina and Katie squealed too.

"You're the first!" Katie exclaimed, and then looked at the others apprehensively. "I mean, I *think* you're the first. Did you guys get your period yet?"

She was relieved when both Trina and Megan solemnly shook their heads. "But I'll bet Erin's got it," Megan said. "She was always saying she's more mature than the rest of us."

"Does it hurt when you get it?" Trina asked Sarah.

"Nah. It's kind of messy, though." Then she grinned. "But it gives me another excuse to get out of hiking and stuff. I can always say I have cramps." She paused thoughtfully. "I wonder if it's possible for a girl to get it every week instead of every month?"

"I don't *think* so," Trina replied. "Hey, here comes Erin. Wow, *she* looks different."

The girls joined her at the window and peered out. Katie barely recognized the girl in tight denim shorts walking slowly up the slope, followed by a uniformed man carrying her suitcase. Even from a distance, she could see that Erin had definitely changed.

"She's got a real figure," Sarah said enviously.

"And look at her hair," Megan murmured. "Do you think those blonde streaks are natural?"

"She didn't have them last year," Katie replied. She watched the girl's approach thoughtfully. Erin was one of those people she would probably never be friendly with back home. First of all, Erin was *very* rich. And secondly, she could be a real snob. But that was one of the most interesting things about camp—you got to be friends with people you never thought you could be friends with.

Erin appeared at the door. "Hi," the girls chorused. This time they didn't scream or hug. That never seemed like the right thing to do with Erin.

"Hi," Erin echoed. She looked around the cabin, and let out a long, mournful sigh. "Same old cabin six."

"Here's your suitcase, Miss Chapman," the uniformed man said, laying it on the single bed.

"Thank you, Peters," Erin said, opening her suitcase. The others exchanged looks. Erin was the only girl they knew who was driven to camp by a chauffeur every summer. Erin pulled a framed picture out of her suitcase and displayed it. "Check this out."

"Who is he?" Katie asked, examining the photograph of a boy with blonde hair hanging in his eyes. He looked older.

"Alan. He's my boyfriend, sort of," Erin said proudly. "And he's thirteen."

"He's cute," Megan said. "Are you allowed to go on dates and everything?"

"Not exactly," Erin admitted. "But we meet at parties. And sometimes I tell my parents I'm going to the movies with a girlfriend, but I'm really meeting him." She sighed deeply. "His parents made him go off to camp this summer, too. It's so gross."

"Aren't you glad to be back here?" Sarah asked.

Erin didn't bother to reply. She just made a face and sank down on her bed.

"I guess you really miss your boyfriend," Megan said sympathetically. "I know *I* would. If I had one, I mean."

"Cheer up, Erin," Katie urged. "You know you'll have fun once things get going around here."

"Fun!" Erin rolled her eyes. "What kind of fun can a girl have when there are no boys around? I wish I could have stayed at home."

"But your boyfriend won't be there," Sarah noted. "You said he was going to camp too."

"So what? There are other boys at home."

Megan shook her head with disapproval. "Oh, Erin, aren't you going to be faithful to him? If you're really truly in love with him, you shouldn't be interested in other boys."

Erin shrugged. "It's just fun to flirt. There's no one here to flirt with."

Katie grinned. "There's always Darrell."

At the mention of the swimming coach, Trina, Megan, and Sarah put their hands over their hearts and sighed deeply. Erin eyed them with scorn. "You guys are *so* immature." She lay back on her bed and closed her eyes.

Katie raised her eyebrows. "Us? Immature?" She started walking backwards toward her bunk bed. "How can you call us immature?" Rapidly, she climbed the ladder and grabbed her pillow. The others recognized the signal, and dashed to their beds for their pillows.

Within two seconds, Erin was being plummeted with pillows. With all the squeals and giggles that followed, no one heard the cabin door open.

Katie saw her first. The tall, fair-haired counselor looked aghast as she took in the sight of four girls pounding another one with pillows. "Girls! What are you doing? Stop this at once!"

All activity ceased as the counselor hurried over to the bed and faced a very disheveled Erin. "Are you all right?"

Erin stared at her blankly. "Of course I'm all right. They're only pillows."

Megan started giggling like a maniac, and the counselor seemed bewildered. "Were these girls picking on you?"

Now Trina looked upset. "Oh no, it's nothing like that. We were just being silly."

Katie realized what the counselor was thinking. There *were* cabins where all the girls ganged up on one poor unfortunate creep. But nothing like that ever happened in six. "We're all friends," she assured the older girl. "We've been together in this cabin for three years. Are you our new counselor?"

The girl looked like she wished she could say no, but she nodded. "I'm Carolyn Lewis." She looked at her watch. "We've got a few minutes before dinner. Why don't we spend some time getting to know each other?"

They all settled down on Erin's bed and introduced themselves. Carolyn repeated each name, as if she was trying to memorize them. She was smiling brightly, but she looked nervous and Katie couldn't blame her. She probably thought she was stuck with a bunch of loonies for the summer.

"And you're all old Sunnyside girls," Carolyn said. "That's nice for me. You see, this is my first year as a counselor, so I'll be counting on you all to show me the ropes."

Katie glanced sideways at Trina, wondering if she was thinking the same thing. A brand-new counselor. This meant they could get away with murder.

"I've been thinking a lot about this job," Carolyn continued, "and I'm really looking forward to getting to know you all. I should probably tell you a little about my philosophy of camp counseling."

The girls stared at her. Since when did a camp counselor need a philosophy, Katie wondered. Erin reached into her suitcase and pulled out a makeup case. From that, she extracted a nail file, and began sliding it across her nails.

"I promise I won't be a dictator," Carolyn told them solemnly. "I believe in group decision making, sharing our goals and objectives. I want you girls to relate to me as a friend, to feel free to express your feelings, your thoughts, and your concerns."

Katie could tell that Megan was trying desperately to stifle a giggle. This one was going to be a pushover.

"We could start right now," Carolyn said. "This being the first day of camp, what are you feeling?"

The girls looked at each other, then back at Carolyn, and shrugged. Carolyn smiled uneasily. "Maybe I should ask you individually. Um, Sarah. What are you feeling right now?"

Sarah gazed at her thoughtfully for a moment before responding. "Hungry."

Now Megan really did giggle. And Katie wasn't able to restrain herself either. Carolyn didn't seem to mind. She smiled. "Well, I guess that makes sense. It *is* time for dinner. I'll just go wash my hands, and we'll go down to the dining hall together." She got up and went to the end of the cabin, where she had her own little room and a private bathroom.

"Is she going to *eat* with us?" Megan asked with horror in her eyes. "Nina stopped eating with us last year. I mean, it's not like we need help cutting our meat or anything."

"I kind of like her," Sarah said. "She's the sensitive type. Maybe if I tell her how much I hate swimming and volleyball, she'll help me get out of it."

"What do you think of her?" Katie asked Trina.

"She seems nice," Trina replied slowly. "Listen, guys, we've got to give her a chance. Let's not do anything mean to her. Not right away, at least."

"I like her hair," Erin commented. "And she's got a good figure. Did you see that pin on her shirt? That's a fraternity pin. It means she has a serious boyfriend and they're almost engaged."

"All ready?" Carolyn emerged from her room. "We have to get there on time. Ms. Winkle's going to make announcements. Uh, have you all washed your hands?"

Katie looked at her evenly. "Carolyn, we're eleven years old. We're not babies."

Carolyn looked stricken. "Oh, I *know* that! I'm truly sorry if I sounded like I was talking down to you. I mean, you're practically teenagers, aren't you? I should have known better than to ask you something like that."

"That's all right," Katie said kindly.

Carolyn twisted her hands. "Well, c'mon, let's go."

As the girls followed her out of the cabin, Katie felt like she'd just scored a major point for the cabin six girls. Of course, they *hadn't* washed their hands. But Carolyn would never ask them a dumb question like *that* again!

* * *

31

The dining hall was in a state of total chaos. Girls were running around all over the place, shouting and laughing and looking for their friends. Shrill shrieks punctuated the air each time someone discovered a buddy she hadn't seen in almost a year.

They always had a particularly good dinner on the first night, and this summer was no exception. Katie happily wolfed down her roast beef and mashed potatoes, pausing every now and then to jump up and greet someone.

As they started on their strawberry shortcake, Ms. Winkle went up on the stage in the front of the room. The whole place broke into applause. Ms. Winkle patted her gray hair and blushed a little.

"Thank you, girls. I'm very happy to see all of you. And I know you're all looking forward to another wonderful summer here at Sunnyside. Before I say anything else, let's start our summer off with a song." She nodded to Ms. Donahue, her assistant, who was sitting at the piano. All the girls rose when she struck up the opening chords of the camp anthem.

"I'm a Sunnyside girl, with a Sunnyside smile,
And I spend my summers in Sunnyside style,
I have sunny, sunny times with my Sunnyside
   friends,
And I know I'll be sad when the summer ends,
But I'll always remember, with joy and pride,
My sunny, sunny days at Sunnyside!"

The room erupted in cheers as the song ended. Katie had to admit it was a pretty silly song, but it still gave her tingles. And she was shocked when she heard Ms. Winkle's next words.

"That may be the last time we sing that song for a while, girls."

A buzz went through the room. The girls at Katie's table looked at one another in bewilderment. "What does she mean?" Trina asked worriedly. "Is the camp closing?"

It couldn't be that, Katie thought. Ms. Winkle looked too happy. And she was obviously enjoying the mystery. She waited for the buzz to die down before she spoke again.

"You see, girls, we're going to have some other campers joining us temporarily. As you know, there are several other camps located in the area around Pine Ridge Lake. One of them, Camp Eagle, suffered a small fire a few days ago. No one was hurt, but it's going to take the camp a week or two to repair the damages. In the meantime, the other camps, including Sunnyside, have volunteered to host the Eagle campers."

Katie still didn't understand what that had to do with the camp song. She found out soon enough.

"So, we've got thirty new campers arriving the day after tomorrow, and we can't very well ask them to sing 'I'm a Sunnyside girl.' Because, you see," and here she paused dramatically. "Our new campers are boys!"

Now the room was *really* buzzing. Across from

Katie, Sarah's mouth fell open. Trina and Megan looked stunned. Only Erin was smiling. Katie sank back in her chair. She was having a hard time absorbing what she had just heard.

Boys. At Sunnyside. The words rang in her ears. She stared at the others in disbelief. Carolyn leaned across the table. "Katie? Are you okay? You look funny."

She *felt* funny. But definitely not funny ha-ha. As a matter of fact, she couldn't even identify what she was feeling. But she knew this—whatever it was she was feeling, it didn't feel good.

Chapter 3

The next morning, Katie paced the floor of the cabin. "We have to do something. We can't let those boys come here."

"Sit down, Katie," Erin ordered. "You're making me nervous."

Katie ignored the command. "You *should* be nervous. Do you know what a bunch of boys could do to this place?"

Megan was sitting on the floor, watching her with wide eyes. "What?"

"Ruin it!" Katie cried out. "I know—I've got brothers. They'll start off by playing dumb tricks, frogs in our beds—that sort of thing. And they'll hog everything—canoes, horses, you name it! They'll take over the whole camp!"

She examined her cabin mates' faces to check out their reactions. Erin looked bored, but that was to be expected—Erin always looked bored. Trina's forehead was puckered, her eyes dark with worry. Sarah was listening intently.

She had definitely gotten through to Megan. The little redhead looked positively frightened. "This is awful," she whispered. "They could really gang up on us." Her eyes glazed over, a clear indication that her imagination was taking off. "We could be out in canoes, and they could tip us over. Or we might be in the pool, and they'll jump us, and hold our heads under water. They could drown us!"

Katie nodded approvingly. Erin just gazed at Megan in disdain. "Darrell would save us."

At the mention of Darrell, Sarah and Trina automatically went into the swooning bit, but it was a halfhearted gesture. Megan was too caught up in her fantasies to notice, and Katie was busy thinking.

"We have to come up with a plan," she said firmly. "We've got one day before the boys arrive. There's still time to convince Ms. Winkle not to let them come."

"I don't know," Trina said slowly. "Maybe we should give the boys a chance. It's just for a couple of weeks."

Katie shook her head. "If we wait till they get here, it'll be too late. Honestly, Trina, I know what boys are like."

"I think Trina's right," Sarah said. "We should wait and see what they're like."

"I'll tell you what they're like," Katie declared. "Sarah, think about volleyball. You know you can never get the ball over the net, so whenever you have to hit it, we always run in front of you and get it over for you, right?"

Sarah nodded.

"Well, a boy would never do that. Boys will just make fun of you for being so weak. They'll laugh and call you names."

Now Sarah was beginning to look nervous.

"I say we have to do something right now to let Ms. Winkle know how we feel about this," Katie stated. "Who agrees with me?"

Megan's hand went up, and a second later, Sarah's followed. Trina looked uncertain, but she finally nodded.

"Erin, what about you?"

Erin yawned. "Personally, I like the idea of having some boys around. There might be a cute thirteen year old in that group."

"There aren't any thirteen year olds," Katie said quickly. "I asked Ms. Donahue after dinner. Only ten and eleven year olds." That wasn't exactly true. Ms. Donahue had only said that most of them were ten and eleven. But she needed all the support she could get, and that meant having Erin on her side.

Erin's face fell with that information. "Oh. *Children.*"

"Erin, *we're* only eleven," Sarah reminded her.

Erin tossed her head. "But everyone knows girls mature faster than boys. These boys will be little kids compared to us."

Katie rewarded her with an emphatic nod. "Okay, then we're all in this together, right?"

"What are we going to do?" Trina asked. "Should we go see Ms. Winkle?"

"No, you know how she is the first week of camp. She'll be too busy to listen to us. Besides, I think we need to make a really strong statement. Something that will get everyone's attention. We have to get all the campers united behind us. Can anyone think of anything?"

"I can't," Sarah said. "I'm too hungry to think. Let's go to breakfast."

"Yeah," Megan echoed. "I'm starving."

Starving. Something clicked in Katie's head. "That's it!" she said. "We'll go on a hunger strike!"

The others gaped at her. "A what?" Trina asked.

"We'll stop eating! And when Carolyn asks us why we're not eating, we'll just say we're refusing to eat if boys come to Sunnyside."

"That's crazy!" Sarah cried out. "We can't starve ourselves to death!"

"We won't have to," Katie assured her. "We'll just refuse to eat breakfast. And when we get to the dining hall, we'll go down the line and tell everyone else to do the same thing. When Ms. Winkle finds out what we're doing, she won't let the boys come!"

"I wouldn't mind going without breakfast," Erin

commented. "I need to lose a couple of pounds anyway."

But no one else looked particularly enthusiastic. "I don't think this can work, Katie," Trina said sadly. "It's too drastic. Ms. Winkle might even call our parents."

"Let's just try it," Katie begged. "It won't hurt to go without one meal."

"Oh yes it will," Sarah argued.

"C'mon, you guys," Katie urged. "Think about those awful boys grabbing our horses and our canoes. We have to take a stand! Even if it doesn't work, at least we'll know we tried."

Trina got up from her bed. "Okay," she said reluctantly. "I'll go along with it. But just for breakfast, okay? Even if Ms. Winkle doesn't change her mind about the boys, we'll still eat lunch, right?"

Katie nodded. "We'll just try something else."

Megan agreed too. Sarah looked totally miserable, but Katie knew she wouldn't go against the group. Just then, Carolyn emerged from her room. "Ready for breakfast?"

Katie winked at the others. "Well, we're ready to *go* to breakfast." They left the cabin together, but the girls walked hurriedly ahead of Carolyn. Along the way, Katie tried to bolster their spirits.

"It won't be so bad," she chattered. "We'll feel good about making a sacrifice for something so important. And they'll probably have something yucky, like those soupy scrambled eggs. And think of Carolyn's face, when we're just sitting there and not eating! She'll freak out!''

But when they walked into the dining hall, a couple of early birds passed them with their trays. And Katie knew it wasn't going to work.

"It's blueberry pancakes," Megan said softly.

"And maple syrup," Sarah said, her expression ecstatic.

"And sausage links," Trina murmured.

Even Katie knew it would be next to impossible to resist Sunnyside's very best breakfast. And from the eager expressions on the faces of the other campers standing on line, she knew it would be totally impossible to convince them to sacrifice.

She'd just have to come up with something else.

The girls got their trays, and joined Carolyn at a table. The conversation turned to the day's activities. There was a volleyball game scheduled for later that morning, and the horses would be arriving that afternoon.

Katie barely listened as the others talked about what they wanted to do. She was busy thinking, trying to figure out what their next step would be. There had to be a way they could convince Ms. Winkle to stop the boys from coming.

Sarah was telling Carolyn about this mysterious skin rash she got whenever she went swimming when Katie got an idea. It was perfect! And this time, everyone would see it.

She was dying to tell the others, but she couldn't in front of Carolyn. Luckily, just then, Teddy the handyman stopped by their table and whispered something to their counselor. She got up. "I'll meet you girls back at the cabin for inspection," she said, and walked off with the handyman.

"I wonder if he's her boyfriend," Erin said, watching them leave the hall.

"Who cares?" Katie said impatiently. "I've got an idea!" She leaned forward and described it. To her satisfaction, they all looked impressed.

"That's fantastic!" Megan squealed. "Ms. Winkle won't be able to ignore *that!*"

"And it's not as if we'd be breaking any rules or anything like that," Trina noted.

"We could do it just before lunch, right here," Sarah added.

Only Erin didn't look too thrilled with the idea. "It sounds like it's going to be embarrassing."

"Not if we stick together," Katie insisted. "But we're going to need lots more girls to make it work. The more, the better." She looked around the room. "Let's see if we can start telling everybody about it now. We've got a few minutes before we have to go back and clean the bunk. Just don't let any of the counselors hear you."

As she joined the others to spread the word, she forgot all about her disappointment over the failure of the hunger strike. The other campers she talked to seemed really interested in her plan. Of course, the little kids were scared. They were afraid Katie's plan would get them into trouble. But the cabin seven girls were all for it.

41

"Sounds great!" one of them exclaimed. "This ought to stir things up!"

Trina reported less success with her tables. "Those cabin nine girls think it's a stupid idea."

"What do you expect?" Katie replied. "They're *twelve*. They probably *like* boys." She didn't care if one or two cabins didn't participate. If the other ones did, they'd have enough to make a real impact. And there was no way Ms. Winkle could ignore it!

Toward the end of their volleyball game, Katie made herself fall down. Trina turned with a look of concern on her face, and Katie winked to let her know she was okay. Then she got up, cupped a hand over her knee, and called out to the counselor who was hurrying toward her. "It's bleeding a little," she lied. "I'm going to get a Band-Aid."

She hobbled off in the direction of the infirmary. As soon as she was out of sight of the volleyball court, she changed direction and ran toward the dining hall. As the leader of this campaign, she figured she ought to get there early.

A group of girls were standing by the hall entrance. They looked like they were around nine or ten. Katie sauntered over to them. "Are you guys going to join us?"

The girls looked at each other and giggled. "We just want to watch. Is that okay?"

"We don't want to get into any trouble," another one piped up.

Before Katie could respond, a voice behind her said, "Hey, are you the one who's trying to keep the boys from coming?"

Katie turned and faced the two older girls standing there. She recognized one of them—Maura, from cabin nine. She was almost thirteen, and acted like she was Miss Sunnyside or something.

Katie nodded. "Yeah. Do you want to help us?"

"Are you crazy?" the other girl asked. "This is the best thing that's happened to this camp ever!"

Katie sighed. She knew the older girls wouldn't go along. "*We* don't think so," she said, wishing her cabin mates would hurry up and get there. "And we're going to do everything we can to stop them from coming."

"Oh yeah?" Maura cocked her head to one side and gave her a look that made Katie distinctly uncomfortable.

"Yeah," Katie shot back, trying to sound a lot more sure of herself than she felt. When she saw Trina and the others running toward her, she felt a lot better. There was definitely strength in numbers.

"Cabin seven's coming," Trina told her breathlessly. "And cabin eight too."

"Great!" Katie exclaimed, tossing a triumphant look at Maura and her friend. In the next few minutes, more girls came to the dining hall. Some just looked curious and stayed away from the entrance. But lots of others, at least thirty, joined the cabin six group, and listened as Katie gave instructions.

"There's Ms. Winkle!" someone yelled. Katie looked up and saw the camp director down the road with a couple of counselors, coming toward the dining hall.

"Where's Erin?" Katie asked. And then she saw her, talking to Maura and some other older girls. "Erin!" she called. Erin pretended not to hear her.

"Maybe this isn't such a great idea," Trina murmured. Her face was already beet red as she watched the approach of Ms. Winkle.

Katie decided they'd better get started immediately before anyone backed out. "Let's go!" she yelled. "No boys at Sunnyside! No boys at Sunnyside!"

Sarah and Megan picked up the chant and formed a line. "No boys at Sunnyside! No boys at Sunnyside!" Trina joined them, and then the rest of the campers formed a ragged line. They started marching back and forth in front of the hall.

Ms. Winkle was getting closer. Katie couldn't tell if she could hear what they were yelling, but she seemed to be walking faster.

"No boys at Sunnyside! No boys at Sunnyside!"

And then, suddenly, someone screamed, "Look!" A big truck was coming up the road. "It's the horses!"

It was as if someone had just yelled Fire! Total pandemonium broke out. Some girls started running after the truck, others cut across a field toward the stables. Megan was jumping up and down. "C'mon, let's go see!"

Katie looked around. Everyone had gone, except for the cabin six gang. And she had to admit, she was dying to see Starfire, the horse she'd ridden all last summer.

Maybe demonstrations weren't the answer, she thought as she raced across the field. She'd just have to come up with something else. But right now, all she could think about was a certain beautiful golden brown mare.

Katie was surprised when Ms. Winkle didn't say a word about the demonstration during the dinnertime announcements. Even though it hadn't lasted very long, she must have gotten a glimpse of it.

She didn't even refer to the boys until the very end of her announcements. "As I told you yesterday, our visitors from Camp Eagle will be arriving tomorrow. Now, I know this will be a new experience for you girls, and some of you may find it uncomfortable having boys here at Sunnyside."

She paused, and looks were exchanged throughout the hall. Ms. Winkle's eyes roamed the room, and Katie had a feeling that every girl who'd taken part in the demonstration thought the director was looking at her.

"But Sunnyside will be doing its part to help our brother camp. And I know you girls will do everything you can to make our visitors feel welcome."

Trina looked at Katie with sympathy in her eyes, and Katie shrugged in resignation. So that was it. The boys were coming and there was nothing they could do about it.

But make them welcome? No way. If nothing else, the Sunnyside girls could make it very clear to the boys that they were not wanted here.

Carolyn left the table to talk to another counselor, and Katie took advantage of her absence. "I've got an idea," she told the others. "We may not be able to keep them out of Sunnyside, but let's let those boys know what we think of them. With any luck, they'll be so miserable here they'll leave."

"How are we going to make them miserable?" Megan asked.

Katie's eyes twinkled wickedly. "First, we have to let them know they're not wanted. When they arrive tomorrow morning, I think we should have signs all over the place telling them just that."

"All over the place?" Sarah repeated.

"Sure!" Katie ticked the places off on her fingers. "On the dining hall, the activities hall, around the swimming pool,—oh, and we'll find out what cabins they're staying in and put them up there." She grinned. "Can't you just imagine their faces tomorrow when they arrive and see the signs? 'Boys Not Wanted!' 'Boys Go Home!' Maybe they won't even get off their bus!"

46

Trina looked troubled. "That's not very nice."

"Of course it's not nice!" Katie replied. "That's the point!"

"But how are we going to make all those signs tonight?" Megan asked.

"We'll get the other kids to help us. Everyone wants to get rid of those boys." She glanced over at the cabin nine table. "Well, almost everyone."

She got up and went over to the cabin seven table. The girls there quickly agreed to help. Then she hit the cabin eight table and got the same response.

"We're all meeting at arts and crafts right after dinner," she reported happily. "The boys might be coming—but I'll bet anything they won't be staying long!"

The arts and crafts counselor, Donna, looked surprised when sixteen girls marched into her cabin.

"Hi!" she greeted them. "What's up?"

The others looked at Katie. She had already prepared what she was going to tell the counselor. And she didn't even have to lie. "We want to make some signs for the camp, to greet the boys who are coming tomorrow." Of course, she didn't tell Donna what kind of greetings.

"What a nice idea!" Donna said. "There's poster paper and markers in the cabinet. Help yourselves."

As the other girls headed to the cabinet, Katie

noticed something that looked like a large doll house on a table. "Is that something for the little kids?" she asked Donna.

"Not exactly," Donna told her. "I thought some of you might like to learn how to make miniature doll house furniture this summer. Furnishing this doll house could be your summer project, if you're interested. Then we could donate it at the end of the summer to the local hospital, for their young patients. Here, let me show you something I made."

In her hand was a tiny chair. Katie admired the detail on the back. It was more like a work of art than a toy. Katie still had her old doll house in her bedroom at home, something her brothers teased her unmercifully about.

"I'd like to learn how to do this," she said.

The others had gathered around her, their arms laden with poster paper. "Where are we going to do this?" one of the cabin eight girls asked.

"How about over at the activities hall?" Megan suggested. "Then we can spread out."

"Do you need any help?" Donna asked.

"No, thanks," Katie called as they ran out of the cabin. She wondered how Donna would feel tomorrow when she saw what the posters said. She felt a little twinge of guilt at the thought, but she shrugged it off. After all, this was important.

The activities hall was empty. Each girl took a piece of poster paper and a marker and got to work. Katie walked around and examined their efforts.

"I don't know what to write," Erin said.

"How about 'We hate boys'?" Sarah suggested.

Trina wrinkled her nose. "That's awfully nasty."

"And not even true," Erin added. "*I* don't hate boys. As long as they're over eleven."

Some of the girls were being really artistic, drawing elaborate borders and making creative statements, like "Sunnyside is an all-girls camp. Are you a girl?" Others were simpler and to-the-point: "No Boys."

A half hour later, they were positioning the posters around the room and admiring them. "This will get rid of them," one of the girls chortled.

Katie hugged herself in glee. And then Carolyn walked into the room. "I've been looking everywhere for you girls," she said to the cabin six gang.

"We have free time after dinner," Katie informed her. "We can do anything we want on the campgrounds."

"I know that," Carolyn said quickly. "I just thought it would be nice if we did something together." Then she noticed the signs, and she frowned. "What's this all about?"

Katie spoke for the group. "We don't want boys coming here. So we're going to put these signs up to let them know how we feel."

Carolyn looked at them seriously. "Why don't you want the boys to come?"

"Because boys are obnoxious," Katie replied promptly.

"And messy and noisy and rude," Megan added.

"It sounds to me like you're making a lot of generalizations," Carolyn said. "Not all boys are obnoxious."

"Carolyn," Sarah said, "didn't you tell us you wanted us to feel free to express our feelings?" When Carolyn nodded, she pointed to the signs. "Well, this is how we're expressing them."

Carolyn sighed. "Listen, guys, I'm tired. Let's talk about this tomorrow, okay?" As she headed toward the door, she turned and said, "Don't forget, you're supposed to be back in the cabin at . . ." her voice trailed off as five pairs of eyes stared at her fixedly. "Well, you know," she finished lamely, leaving the room.

As soon as she was gone, Katie turned to the others. "We've got to get these up all over camp, tonight, so the boys will see them as soon as they arrive."

One of the cabin seven girls stared at her. "You mean, we have to sneak out after hours?"

"It's the only way," Katie told her. "I figure the boys will be arriving for breakfast." She checked her watch. "Let's meet back here at eleven. Everyone should be in bed by then."

Megan, sitting on the floor, giggled and hugged

her knees to her chest. "Our first real camp adventure!"

They piled the posters up in a corner, and the girls separated to go back to their cabins. "Do you really think this is going to work?" Sarah asked Katie as they headed toward cabin six.

"I have no doubt about it," Katie declared. "Now we all have to stay awake till eleven."

It wasn't that difficult. Everyone was too excited to sleep. Sarah had brought a pack of cards with her, and they played Go Fish. Even Erin joined in, all the while complaining about doing something so babyish. Luckily, Carolyn didn't check to see if their lights were out.

At precisely eleven, they turned out the lights and filed silently out the door. They didn't even whisper as Katie led them down to the path leading to the activities hall.

The campgrounds were silent. As they made their way in the darkness, clutching hands, Katie shivered in the warm night air. This was what being a Sunnyside girl was all about—united with your cabin mates, working toward a goal together. She felt positively giddy.

In the activities hall, the other girls were waiting. Katie assigned each group places to stick up their posters and handed out thumbtacks. Then they gathered the posters and took off.

The cabin six girls had the dining hall. As silently as possible, they stuck the posters all over the outside walls. They used their sneakers to pound the thumbtacks in quietly. Then they stepped back to examine their efforts.

"Wow," Megan breathed. Her voice was barely above a whisper, but the others hushed her anyway. Katie motioned for them to follow her back. They couldn't hang around to admire their work. Besides, they couldn't read the words in the darkness anyway. Tomorrow, in the morning light, the words would be clear for everyone to see.

Chapter 4

But the next morning, when the girls went down to the dining hall for breakfast, they stared in silent dismay at the blank walls. A couple of girls from cabin eight joined them.

"They're gone from the cabins, too," one of them announced. "It looks like someone took them all down."

"Probably Ms. Winkle," Katie said. Well, at least the camp director got their message, even if they didn't get a chance to share it with the new arrivals.

Other campers gathered around Katie. "Now what are we going to do?"

Katie didn't have the slightest idea, but she wasn't about to admit it. "I've got a plan," she lied. "I'll spread the word during breakfast. That is, if we get any breakfast. They're probably already in there, eating ours."

But there weren't any new campers in the dining hall, and Katie felt a sudden rush of hope.

Maybe, after seeing the signs, Ms. Winkle had called Camp Eagle and cancelled the boys.

But no such luck. When Ms. Winkle made her morning announcements, she told them about the hours that the ice cream stand would be open. She announced a trip on Saturday into Pine Ridge, and a movie by the lake on Saturday night. And she told them the boys would be arriving after breakfast. She didn't actually mention the signs, but it was soon clear that she had seen them.

"I realize that some of you aren't happy about this. But I'm trusting in the Sunnyside spirit of cooperation and sharing. While the boys are here, they're going to be using our facilities, our horses, our canoes—and this may mean an occasional sacrifice on your part. I do believe that Sunnyside girls will meet this challenge with a smile, and refuse to have anything to do with hostile acts against the boys."

Katie stared down at her soggy cereal. Now what? When she raised her eyes, she saw Carolyn looking at her meaningfully.

"I want you girls to promise me you won't do anything nasty to the boys," she said. She was speaking to the whole group but her eyes were fixed on Katie.

Katie glanced around at her cabin mates. They were all looking at her. She turned back to Carolyn. "What do you mean, 'nasty'?" she asked.

"Nasty," Carolyn said again. "Like pulling pranks on them. Or making more signs." She paused. "You know, I didn't tell Ms. Winkle who made those signs."

Katie raised her eyebrows. She'd been wondering about that, and from the others' expressions, she could tell they'd been worried too. No one wanted demerits this early in the summer.

"So you owe me a favor," Carolyn continued. "Promise me you won't do anything to the boys."

For a moment, Katie resisted. If they didn't do anything to drive the boys away, they'd stay until it was time for them to go back to Eagle. And then she had an idea.

"Okay. We promise. I mean, if that's okay with you guys."

The other girls nodded, but they were looking at her with surprise. It wasn't like Katie to give up so easily.

But what they didn't know yet was that she hadn't given up. True, they wouldn't do anything nasty to the boys.

They just wouldn't have anything to do with them at all.

She didn't have a chance to share her idea right away. Carolyn stayed with them all through breakfast and walked back to the cabin with them. She had just gone into her room when Megan, looking out the window, gave a shout. "I see a bus!"

Erin joined her at the window and peered out at

the distant road. She squinted to read the words on the side of the bus. "Camp Eagle."

"That's them," Katie said, pounding her pillow flat with more energy than usual.

Trina emerged from the lower bed and looked up. "Cheer up. They won't be here forever. Like Ms. Winkle said, it's just until they finish making repairs at Camp Eagle."

Katie swung her legs over the side of the bed and hopped down. "But who knows how long that's going to take? Last year, my parents had to have the garage door repaired. The man who was fixing it said it would take two days. It ended up taking a week! Those boys could end up staying here all summer!"

"Maybe they won't like it here," Sarah said. She was sitting on the side of her bed in her bathing suit, carefully applying red dots to her left knee with a marking pen. "And if they don't like Sunnyside, maybe they'll just go home."

Erin watched her with interest. "Sarah, what are you doing?"

Sarah didn't look up. She was concentrating on her right knee now. "I'm making a rash. When Darrell sees it, he'll tell me I can't go in the water."

"If you're not going swimming, why are you wearing a bathing suit?" Trina asked.

"Because this way, it'll look like I *want* to go swimming. And when Darrell says I can't, I'll pretend to be really disappointed."

Trina crossed the room to examine Sarah's work. She shook her head doubtfully. "I hate to tell you this, Sarah, but that doesn't look like a real rash. Katie, come here and look."

But Katie wasn't listening. Now was the time to announce her plan. "You know what? We can make *sure* they don't like Sunnyside."

The others looked at her curiously. "What do you mean?" Megan asked.

"We promised Carolyn we wouldn't do anything nasty," Trina reminded her.

Katie hopped up on the windowsill. "We don't have to do anything nasty. We can ignore them, just pretend they don't even exist. And we can refuse to have anything to do with them."

"You mean, not speak to them at all?" Sarah asked.

"Well, if they try to push ahead in line at the dining hall, we can say stuff like 'Cut it out.' We just won't say anything nice or friendly." She jumped down from the windowsill. "Let's make a vow."

"Oh, come on," Erin complained. "That's kid stuff."

Katie ignored that comment. "How does this sound? We, the girls of cabin six, vow to have nothing to do with any boys at Sunnyside." Then, in the cabin six tradition, she went around the room and slapped palms with each girl. When she got to Erin's bed, Erin didn't look at her, and she didn't raise her palm.

"Erin, are you with us or not?"

"This is so dumb," Erin muttered. Katie just stood there, waiting, her hand up.

"Okay," Erin said finally, with a big show of reluctance. She raised her hand listlessly. "I mean, it's not as if I want to have anything to do with little boys."

Carolyn came out of her room. "All ready for inspection?" she asked cheerfully. The girls went to their own beds and stood beside them. When Carolyn got to Sarah and Megan's area, she seemed more interested in Sarah than her bed.

"Sarah, what's that on your knees? Is that some sort of new fad or something?" While Megan stifled a giggle, Sarah gazed wide-eyed at Carolyn.

"It's that rash I get. I just hope Darrell doesn't see it. I don't want to miss swimming!" Carolyn raised her eyebrows, but she didn't say anything. And the girls were dismissed to go to the pool.

Erin was the first to spot the boys. There were four of them, coming up the path, and all wearing Camp Eagle shorts and tee shirts. "Hey," Erin whispered to the others. "They don't look so young!"

"Don't even look at them!" Katie hissed. The boys were getting closer. The cabin six girls kept their eyes focused straight ahead. When they were directly passing, one of the boys grinned, and another said, "Hi." But the girls didn't even acknowledge them.

Except for Erin. She didn't speak, but she

turned to look back at them after they passed. And one of them turned to look at her. "Erin!" Sarah said. "Remember, you took a vow!"

"But he's *cute!*" Erin exclaimed. "And he looks at least twelve, maybe even thirteen!"

Katie looked at her seriously. "Erin, we have to stick together. And you know that loyalty to your cabin comes before everything else."

Erin made a face but she didn't argue. And then Sarah let out a soft shriek. "Oh no! Look, you guys! There's more of them at the pool!"

Sure enough, there were five boys horsing around by the side of the pool. They looked like they were trying to push each other in. On the other side of the pool, the girls from cabin seven were watching them and giggling. Katie made a mental note to tell them the new plan of action. She knew from experience that giggling at boys only made them show off more.

"Just ignore them," she ordered the others. "We're going to have to pass them, but just stay as close to the pool as possible. Pretend they have cooties."

Megan giggled. "They probably do."

"Cooties!" Erin gazed at them in dismay. "I can't believe how immature you guys are! I haven't used that word since third grade!"

The girls formed a single line and edged along the side of the pool. Just as they were passing the boys, one of them pushed another one, whose arm swung out and hit Sarah. Sarah promptly lost her balance and crashed into the pool.

"Sarah!" Trina cried out. They all knew Sarah couldn't swim. Katie was prepared to jump in after her when Sarah's head emerged. Luckily, it was the shallow end. And Sarah wasn't hurt, just stunned. She stood there, up to her waist in water, and glared at the boys.

"Sorry," one of them called down to her. His freckled face actually did look apologetic. But Katie knew that look. She'd seen it on her brothers' faces, whenever they thought they might be in real trouble.

"You *should* be sorry," Megan snapped at him.

"Don't even talk to them," Katie whispered. "Act like they're not even there." She knelt by the side of the pool and helped Sarah get out.

"Oh, no," Sarah moaned as she grabbed Katie's hand and hoisted herself up. "My rash is gone." She gazed down in sorrow at her knees, which the water had washed clean.

Two of the cabin seven girls came over. "Are you okay?" one asked Sarah.

"Did you see what those boys did?" Katie asked. "They pushed her in on purpose!" The cabin seven girls looked horrified.

"I thought it was an accident," Sarah started to say, but Katie didn't let her finish. Quickly, she explained their plan to have nothing to do with the boys.

"We'll spread the word," the cabin seven girls promised.

Darrell blew his whistle and joined them. "Okay, kids, let's get going. This summer, we're going to work on drown-proofing."

"What's that?" Trina asked.

"It's learning how to save yourself if you're ever in danger of drowning," the handsome swimming coach explained.

"I already know a way to do that," Sarah told him. "Never get near any water."

Darrell grinned good-naturedly. "We'll make a fish out of you yet, Sarah. Now, first of all, everyone needs a partner, someone of approximately the same height."

The six girls from cabin seven immediately paired themselves off while Darrell addressed the cabin six girls. "Megan, you're with Sarah, Trina with Erin. Katie, you can pair off with—what's your name?"

"Justin," replied the freckle-faced, red-haired boy.

Katie looked at Darrell in horror. "Forget it!"

"What's the problem?" Darrell asked.

"I'm *not* going to be partners with a boy!"

Justin didn't look too thrilled either. The other boys were laughing and poking him.

"Look," Darrell said, "everyone has to have a partner for drown-proofing. And there aren't any more girls."

Katie didn't say anything. She stood there resolutely, folded her arms across her chest, and gave her head a firm shake. Just then, Sarah let out a little cry. She put her hand over her eyes, and started swaying.

"Now what's *your* problem?" Darrell asked. He was starting to sound impatient.

"I'm a little dizzy," Sarah said weakly. "I think maybe I got too much water in my ears when I fell in."

"When you were *pushed* in," Katie corrected her.

"Yeah. Maybe I'd better just watch today."

Darrell raised his eyes to the heavens and shook his head wearily. "All right, Katie, you can be with Megan."

Katie shot a grateful look at Sarah, and glanced at Justin. He was staring out at the pool, and his face was almost as red as his hair. This was perfect, Katie thought. They'd made a point, and the red-haired boy must have gotten the message. With Sarah's collection of excuses, it could be days before she had to go swimming and Darrell tried to pair them off again. And by then, maybe all the boys would have gotten the message—and left.

Katie was humming as she walked to the arts and crafts cabin. The word had spread throughout the camp, and everything was working out nicely. The girls had stood together in volleyball, flatly refusing to have any boys on their teams, despite the pleas of the counselor. And she'd heard through the grapevine that a girl from cabin five had refused to share a canoe with a boy.

Now it was free time, and Katie was going to work on the dollhouse. She'd gotten started earlier that day, in the regular arts and crafts session, and Donna had promised to teach her some new things if she came around during free time.

The cabin was busy. At one table, a counselor was showing some little kids how to make pot holders. A group at another table were making belts. Katie headed toward the back of the cabin, where the dollhouse was standing. And then she stopped dead in her tracks.

"Hey!" she called. "What are you doing with that? Put it down!"

It was Justin from the pool, and he was handling the little table she'd worked on that morning. Donna emerged from the storage closet and came toward them. "Katie, have you met Justin?"

Katie put her hands on her hips and didn't say anything. Donna didn't seem to notice her expression, though. "He's interested in miniature furniture too. And I'm really glad, because I can't find many kids who want to get involved. I thought you two could work together on this. You could show him what I taught you this morning."

Katie looked at Justin in disbelief. She'd never heard of a boy working on a dollhouse. He probably has some rotten trick in mind, she thought. Like fixing the furniture so it will come apart when anyone touches a piece.

"I already know how to do a lot of this stuff," Justin informed Donna. "I made furniture for my little sister's dollhouse."

Katie hoped her expression revealed what she was thinking: he's a liar. Whoever heard of an older brother doing something really nice for a kid sister?

Justin eyed Katie narrowly. "I could show you how to do hinges."

"No thanks," Katie replied coldly. "I don't work with boys." She turned to Donna. "I'll come back when he's not here." She turned and marched out of the cabin.

Her cheerful mood had vanished. She'd been looking forward to working on that dollhouse. And now that creep had ruined it for her.

"Katie!" Megan came running toward her, carrying a tennis racket. "Want to go play tennis?"

"No thanks." She wasn't in the mood. Besides, she was pretty crummy at tennis, and Megan was good. Playing tennis seemed to be about the only time she didn't daydream.

Megan's face fell. "I can't get anyone to play with me."

Katie tried to be sympathetic. "That's because you're the only tennis nut in cabin six, and none of us are as good at it as you are."

"You're right," Megan said. She wasn't being very modest, but it was true. Megan took tennis lessons at home and she was a better player than anyone at camp. "I wish I could find someone around here who's on the same level. You want to get some ice cream?"

Katie agreed, and they headed for the stand. Erin was there by herself, licking a frozen yogurt, and watching some boys who were sitting on the grass nearby.

"That dark-haired one is so cute," she told Katie and Megan. "He's almost as cute as my boyfriend back home."

"Now, Erin," Megan said, "how would you feel if you knew your boyfriend was looking at other girls right this minute?"

Erin shrugged and grinned. "He probably is. His camp's coed." The dark-haired boy looked up and met Erin's eyes. Erin pushed her hair back and smiled slightly.

"Erin!" Katie exclaimed. "Knock it off! Remember, you promised to go along with us."

Erin made a face at her. But she turned away from the boys and sat on the grass with Katie and Megan. When they finished their ice cream, Megan got up. "There's still a half hour left of free time. I'm going to go hang around the tennis court and see if I can find someone to play with."

Erin got up too. "I want to wash my hair before dinner."

Katie looked at her suspiciously. "Why?"

Erin shrugged. "Maybe I just want to look nice. Is there any law against that?" She walked off toward their cabin, and Megan headed down to the tennis court.

Katie decided to go to the stables. Other cabins had horseback riding now, but maybe no one was on Starfire and she could have a quick ride before dinner.

Jerry, one of the stable hands, was brushing a small pony as Katie approached. "Hi, Jerry," she called out.

He waved back. "How're ya doing, Katie? Take a look at this little honey. Isn't she a knockout?"

Katie admired the pony. For the next few minutes, she talked horses with Jerry. He was one of her favorite people at Sunnyside. It was funny to think that obnoxious boys could grow up to be neat people like Jerry or Darrell or that nice handyman, Teddy.

"Is Starfire free?" she asked him.

Jerry shook his head. " 'Fraid not. Someone's saddling her right now."

Katie sighed. This wasn't her day. "I'll just go in and say hello to her."

She was on her way down to Starfire's stall, when the mare emerged. And then Katie felt her face start to burn. Holding on to Starfire's reins and leading her out was Justin.

"What are you doing with my horse!" she yelled.

The boy faced her defiantly. "Since when is this *your* horse? She belongs to the camp."

"Right," Katie shot back. "And this is *my* camp. Not yours."

Justin's freckles started to blend as his face

went pink. "Gee, you really know how to make a guy feel welcome."

For some crazy reason, Katie had a sudden memory flash—a birthday party she'd gone to when she was eight. The birthday girl had gotten into a fight with some other kid. "I didn't want you to come," she'd yelled. "My mother made me invite you." Katie could still see the hurt look on that little kid's face.

Of course, Justin didn't look like that. He just looked angry. But then he extended the reins to Katie. "If she means that much to you, you can have her."

Katie stared at him in bewilderment. This guy was definitely strange. She drew herself up straight.

"I don't want to ride her now," she said stiffly. "You probably saddled her all wrong anyway." It was a pretty dumb thing to say, but it was all she could think of for the moment. And holding her head high, she turned and left the stable.

Chapter 5

"Why don't they leave?" Katie grumbled to Trina as they pushed their way through some bushy foliage in the woods behind the campgrounds. She'd gone on this nature walk in hopes of getting away from boys for a little while. But three of them had joined the group, including that creepy Justin who seemed to be everywhere Katie went.

"They've only been here three days," Trina reminded her. "I guess they haven't gotten the message yet."

Katie wondered if they ever would. One of the cabin seven girls had discovered that one of the boys was her cousin. She had to talk to him or it would get back to her parents and they'd have a fit. And another boy had helped a cabin eight girl when she fell off a horse and broke her ankle. She had to say thanks.

Most of the girls were still staying away from the boys. But the big wave of enthusiasm that had greeted Katie's campaign had worn off. She almost wished the boys would act worse to keep the girls stirred up against them.

"Where's Megan?" Trina asked suddenly.

Katie looked back to where the counselor had stopped the group. She was giving her lecture on the types of trees in the woods. Katie had heard it before, so she and Trina had pushed on ahead.

"She's probably still sitting on that rock back there, daydreaming," she said.

"Look!" Trina clutched Katie's arm. "There's a deer!"

Katie peered through the leaves in the direction Trina was pointing. "Oh," she whispered softly. "It's so beautiful."

Behind her, the others were coming around the bend. Katie turned to them, beckoned, and put a finger to her lips. "Shh! There's a deer out here!"

The group became instantly quiet, and some tiptoed closer to gather around Katie and Trina. There was total silence as they all held their breath and admired the graceful creature poised on the edge of a path.

A boy jostled Katie aside in order to get a better look. "Hey! It's Bambi!" At the sound of his loud, jeering voice, the deer took off.

"Now what did you do that for?" Trina asked him sadly.

The boy didn't answer. He was too busy laughing hysterically with another boy. Katie answered for him.

"He did it because he's a boy and boys do stupid things like that." She said it loudly, hoping the other girls in the group would pick up the cry. One of them nodded, and another one wrinkled her nose, but nobody seemed particularly angry. They moved on ahead up the trail.

"See?" Katie said to Trina. "They ruin everything! Every time I want to work on the dollhouse in arts and crafts, that Justin's there. And the other day, he was riding Starfire. I almost didn't come on this walk when I saw him here."

"Which one is he?" Trina asked, looking up ahead at the rest of the campers.

Katie couldn't see him in the group. She looked around uneasily. "He's probably hiding behind a bush, waiting to jump out and scare us or something. That's the kind of thing my brothers would do."

The counselor came back, and motioned for them to join the others. "C'mon, girls, I want to do a head count." Katie and Trina followed her up the ridge. As the counselor counted heads, she frowned. At the same time, Trina was looking around anxiously.

"Megan's not here!"

"Someone else is missing too," the counselor said.

"It's Justin," one of the boys told her.

"I think I know where Megan is," Katie told the counselor. "I'll go get *her*." She wanted to make it clear that Megan was the only one she'd look for. Because if she saw Justin, she'd just as soon let him stay lost.

She hurried back down the trail toward the big rock. Megan wasn't there, though. Katie noticed another trail, going off the opposite way. She figured Megan probably lost her sense of direction and took that one. She hurried down the trail.

"Megan!" she called.

A voice responded, but it definitely wasn't Megan's. "Hey! Over here!"

It was a boy's voice. Katie debated ignoring it, but maybe he'd found Megan. She followed the sound, and located the source behind a cluster of large oak trees, beside a creek. And then she groaned. Megan wasn't there. It was only Justin.

Katie put her hands on her hips and gazed at him with disdain. "Are you lost?"

The red-haired boy looked uncomfortable as he met her eyes. "No, I'm not lost," he retorted. "I, uh, just wanted to get a closer look at these plants." He held up a hand clutching shiny green leaves. "I'm interested in plants, if it's any of your business."

Katie glanced at the leaves he was holding, and her eyes widened. She stifled a giggle. "Well, those are certainly very interesting leaves you have there. Would you like to know what they're called?"

The boy eyed her narrowly. "What?"

Katie smirked. "Poison ivy."

Justin yelped, and dropped the leaves. Katie

couldn't restrain her giggles any longer. "Feeling a little itchy?" she asked.

Justin glared at her. Then his eyes fell, and suddenly he was grinning. "Not yet. How about you?"

Katie looked down. Then *she* yelped. She was standing in a clump of the very same leaves. She leaped out of it, and Justin started laughing. Katie stamped her foot. "It's all your fault," she yelled. "Why don't you boys go back where you came from?" She turned and headed back toward the main trail. She could hear Justin following her, but she ignored him.

When she reached the others, she saw Megan, who had drifted back on her own. "Oh good," the counselor said to Katie. "You found Justin." Trina and Megan looked at Katie in surprise.

"I didn't really talk to him," Katie assured them. "I just told him to go back where he came from." Trina and Megan nodded understandingly.

For the rest of the nature walk, they managed to avoid any more encounters with boys. And as soon as they were out of the woods, they raced back to cabin six for Erin. It was their turn to take canoes out. But Ms. Winkle had told them there might not be enough canoes to go around, and they wanted to get to the lake before the boys had a chance to grab them all.

But only Sarah was in the cabin, curled up on her bed and reading. "Where's Erin?" Katie asked her.

Sarah looked up from her book. "I don't know.

72

She took off right after you guys left and she hasn't been back."

"I told her to meet us back here," Trina said. "I guess we'd better wait for her."

"If we wait, we won't get canoes," Megan reminded her.

"We'll have to go without her," Katie decided. "It's her own fault for being late."

"But then there's only three of us," Trina objected. "And it's two to a canoe. They won't let one person in a canoe alone." All eyes turned to Sarah, who'd gone back to her book.

"Sarah," Megan wheedled, "want to go canoeing?"

Sarah glanced up briefly. "Nope."

In unison, the other three chorused, "Please?" "If you don't come with us, one of us won't get to go," Trina said.

Sarah made a face. Katie knew she hated being on top of the water as much as she hated being in it. But she also knew that Sarah could be counted on to come through for cabin six.

"C'mon, Sarah," she urged. "We really want to go. Don't let us down like Erin did. We need you."

Sarah sighed, but loyalty won out over fear of water. With a look of regret, she laid down her book. "Okay. But if I fall in, do you all promise to jump in and rescue me?"

They all agreed, and took off for the lake. "You know, Sarah," Trina said, "if you learned to swim, you wouldn't have to worry so much about drowning."

"But if I just stay out of the water, I don't have to worry about drowning," Sarah replied.

"You'd probably like swimming if you tried it," Megan told her as they ran down the hill to the banks of the lake. Sarah looked like she was about to argue, but her attention was distracted.

"Hey, look! That boy's trying to take a canoe by himself!"

The boy had already dragged the canoe into the water. A girl sitting on the banks called out to him. "Hey, you're not allowed to take a canoe alone."

"Okay," the boy called back. "You want to come with me?"

Katie gasped as the girl stood up. Was she actually going to do it? Then the girl saw Katie and the others. She turned back to the boy. "No, thanks. I don't get into canoes with boys." She sauntered away. The boy stared after her for a minute, and then pulled the canoe back onto the shore.

Katie allowed herself a small, triumphant smile. The campaign was still happening.

"There's Erin," Megan said. "What's she doing?"

Erin was standing by a canoe. On the other side of it was the dark-haired boy she'd been eyeing. "She's probably fighting him for the canoe," Megan said. "C'mon, let's help her out."

74

Erin didn't look particularly pleased to see them. "Oh, hi," she murmured. She glanced back at the boy, who winked at her.

Katie glanced at him suspiciously, and then spoke to Erin. "Let's go get a canoe."

"But there's already four of you," Erin said quickly. "And we can't get three in a canoe."

"I'll just watch," Sarah offered cheerfully. "I don't mind."

Erin's eyes darted back and forth between the girls and the boy. Then she put her hands on her hips, and faced the girls decisively. "I just told Bobby I'd canoe with him."

Katie's mouth fell open. The other three looked just as stunned. "Erin!" Katie exclaimed. "We made a vow!"

"Oh, don't be so juvenile," Erin said airily. She turned back to the boy. "Let's go." The two of them began to push the canoe out into the water. The girls watched them in disbelief.

"Oh, Erin," Trina moaned. "How could you do this?" But Erin couldn't hear her. She and the boy had climbed into the canoe and were paddling away.

"She betrayed us," Katie said in hushed tones.

"Here come some more boys," Megan announced suddenly. "We better grab those two canoes." They ran for them, and in unspoken agreement, pushed them in the opposite direction of Erin and her new friend. For a moment, they were occupied with getting settled, Trina and Katie in one canoe, Megan and Sarah in the other. They paddled alongside each other in silence for a few minutes.

"I can't believe Erin's doing that," Sarah remarked, slapping the water lightly with her oar. "We've always stood together before."

"Erin's changed," Trina said sadly.

"No kidding," Megan declared. "I mean, she was always a little stuck up. But now she's acting really snotty."

Katie was deep in thought. She was very upset. In past summers, the girls had argued, even fought about things. But they were always loyal in the end. This was the first time a cabin six girl had become a traitor. "What are we going to do about her?" she asked the others.

"We could short sheet her bed," Sarah suggested halfheartedly.

"That's not enough," Megan objected. "It has to be something bigger than that."

There was a moment of silence as they contemplated an appropriate punishment. "If she's not going to be loyal to cabin six," Katie said finally, "then we're just going to have to act like she's not even there."

"You mean, not speak to her at all?" Trina asked. Katie nodded.

"If she wants to hang out with boys, then we'll treat her like we treat the boys."

"That makes sense," Sarah said.

Trina and Megan agreed, but Trina gazed wistfully across the lake at Erin's canoe. "I wish things could be the way they used to be."

Katie nodded solemnly. It was going to be awful in the cabin, with everyone ignoring Erin. But she'd broken her vow. And now she had to pay the price.

The next morning, half asleep, Katie rubbed her left ankle with her right foot. It didn't help. Suddenly, she was completely awake. And itching. She tossed off her blanket, and examined her left ankle. "Oh no!"

Erin sat up in bed. "What's the matter?"

Katie opened her mouth, and then snapped it shut. She'd almost forgotten that Erin didn't exist, not as far as the rest of cabin six was concerned.

Trina had heard her too. Her head appeared on the side of Katie's bed. "What's going on?"

Glumly, Katie pointed to her ankle. The red spots were faint, but Katie knew from experience they'd be bright before long. And itching even worse than they did now.

Trina echoed her reaction. "Oh no. How did you get poison ivy?"

"When I went looking for Megan yesterday. I just hope that jerk Justin got it too. Only worse."

By now, Sarah and Megan were stirring, and a moment later they were standing on the edge of Trina's bed, looking at Katie's ankle. "Lucky

77

you," Sarah said enviously. "You won't be able to go in the pool."

Katie grimaced. "I *like* swimming, Sarah. Maybe no one will notice." But just then, Carolyn emerged from her room. Seeing the girls gathered around Katie, she joined them before Katie could pull over a sheet to cover the rash.

"That looks like poison ivy," she said.

"No, it isn't," Katie said quickly. "It doesn't even itch." But even as she spoke, the urge to scratch was overwhelming. And she had to give in.

"You better get right down to the infirmary," Carolyn said. "Maybe they can do something to keep it from spreading."

"Okay," Katie replied reluctantly. "I guess Darrell would have noticed it too."

"I'm going into the showers," Erin announced from the other side of the room. No one responded. Erin shrugged, and went into the bathroom. She knew what was going on, but she was pretending it didn't bother her.

Then something occurred to Katie. "What are you going to do about drown-proofing?" she asked Trina. "You're supposed to be her partner."

Trina bit her lower lip. "I guess I could be her partner without talking to her."

"I think you should ask for a new partner," Megan stated.

Carolyn was listening curiously. "Why don't you want to be Erin's partner?"

Katie was trying to pull on her shorts and scratch her ankle at the same time. The others waited for her to answer Carolyn. Katie decided to tell the truth. Carolyn might as well know where they stood.

"Because she's hanging out with boys. And we promised each other we wouldn't have anything to do with them."

Carolyn frowned. "Katie! You promised me you guys wouldn't do anything nasty to the boys!"

"We're not doing anything nasty. We're just ignoring them. And they deserve to be ignored."

Trina tried to explain. "It's because of a boy that Katie got poison ivy. And two guys splashed us yesterday when we were out in the canoes."

"They were probably just trying to have fun with you," Carolyn said. "I'll bet you girls splash each other all the time."

Katie had to admit this was true. In fact, the girls usually tried to tip each other's canoes over. But Carolyn didn't need to know this.

Sarah and Megan offered more evidence. "The boys were hogging the tennis courts yesterday," Megan told her.

"And they took all the brownies at dinner last night," Sarah complained. "I couldn't even get seconds."

Carolyn looked a little more sympathetic. "I know the camp is more crowded than usual. But they'll be gone in a week. Just try to make the best of it, okay?" She went back to her room to get dressed, and the girls looked at each other in dismay.

"Another whole week," Sarah groaned. "Can't we think of something to do to get rid of them faster?"

All Katie could think about was her itchy ankle. "I'm going to the infirmary. I'll see you guys in archery."

By the time she got to the infirmary, her ankle was itching even more. And when she walked in, she saw with a sinking heart that she wouldn't get relief right away. There were six other campers ahead of her. She got a small sense of satisfaction in noticing that one of them was Justin.

Their eyes met for a second, and then they both looked away. Katie sat down as far from him as possible. One by one, each camper was called in to the treatment room. Finally, the only ones left were Katie and Justin.

Justin broke the silence. "I got it worse than you."

Katie glanced out of the corner of her eye. Despite herself, she couldn't help feeling a little sorry for him. The rash was on the palm of his hand and halfway up his arm.

"I'm not going to be much good at making doll furniture for a while," he said. Katie stared fixedly straight ahead. "Sorry you had to get it too," he added.

Katie looked at him in surprise. Was he actually apologizing?

He seemed encouraged by her look. "If I hadn't called out yesterday, you wouldn't have stepped into the stuff."

Katie wanted to say "You're absolutely right," but she held it back. Maybe he really was sorry. She acknowledged his statement with a brief nod, and looked away.

"Hey. What do you have against me, anyway?"

Katie was taken aback. Justin was looking at her seriously, almost sadly. She decided she might as well answer. There was no one else in there to hear her.

But she spoke as coldly as possible. "It's nothing personal. We just don't want boys at Sunnyside."

"You think we want to be here?" Justin asked. "If it wasn't for that dumb fire, we'd be across the lake at Eagle right now, having a great time." His voice grew louder, and his tone got angrier. "Instead, we've all been separated. And my group got stuck at a camp where hardly anyone even talks to us."

Katie stared at him in astonishment. He actually sounded upset. His face was beet red. "It isn't our fault we're here! And everyone's treating us like we're an invading army or something! And I'll bet you're the one who started it all."

Katie didn't know what to do. She'd promised to ignore the boys and pretend they didn't even exist. But this one . . . he actually seemed sincere.

Maybe it wouldn't hurt just to give him an explanation.

"See, I've got brothers. Two of them, twins. And they drive me crazy. They tease me and pick on me and play dirty tricks. I was looking forward to being in a place where there's no boys. And then you guys showed up."

Some of the red was leaving his face. He was looking at her with interest. "I've got a kid sister. And she drives me crazy."

"But I'll bet you're worse to her," Katie accused him.

He looked like he was trying not to smile, but he couldn't quite manage it. "Sometimes."

The both fell silent. Then Justin said, "Look, I really want to work on that doll furniture. Only I can't do everything because of my hand. You want to work together on it this afternoon in arts and crafts? And during free time too?"

Katie looked at him in confusion. Maybe he was different. Maybe he wasn't as awful as her brothers. And she did want to work on the furniture. But how could she? She'd made a vow. She couldn't betray her cabin mates, like Erin did.

Justin went on. "Donna says if she doesn't get more people working on the dollhouse, it won't be ready to give to the hospital at the end of the summer."

Katie chewed on a fingernail. She still didn't know what to say. Luckily, she was spared having to come up with an immediate answer. Justin got called in to the treatment room.

Alone in the waiting room, Katie debated. Justin could be putting on a big act. He might be trying to get her to work on the furniture just so he could sabotage her work. On the other hand, maybe not. And, she really wanted to work on the dollhouse.

But here she was, the leader of the anti-boy campaign. What if the others found out she was working with a boy? She'd be in total disgrace. They'd be even angrier at her than they were at Erin. No one, not even Trina, would speak to her. She'd be dead meat.

But maybe . . . maybe she could work it out so they didn't have to know. Was she willing to take that risk?

Justin emerged from the treatment room, his arm spread thickly with lotion. The nurse beckoned for Katie to come in.

"Well?" Justin asked as she passed him. "Are you going to work with me?"

Katie made a decision. "Okay. But if anyone else is in there, we can't talk, okay? I can tell the others Donna's making us work together. But I have to act like I don't want to be doing it."

Justin nodded. "I understand. The other guys would give me a hard time too."

There was an awkward pause. "Guess I'll see you later, then," Katie said.

"Yeah," Justin replied.

Katie went on into the treatment room, and sat silently on the examining table, dimly aware of the doctor looking at her ankle. What had she just gotten herself into? Was she crazy? What if the others found out? Maybe Erin could handle the silent treatment, but Katie knew *she* couldn't.

I'm doing this so the kids in the hospital can have a dollhouse, she told herself firmly. But she wondered if the other girls would believe that. Or if they'd just consider her another traitor.

She was just going to have to be very, very careful, and make absolutely, positively sure they never found out.

She met the rest of the group at archery. Sarah was looking frazzled, which surprised Katie. Archery was the only activity she liked, because you didn't have to move around so much.

"What's up?" she asked, as she strung her bow.

"Drown-proofing," Sarah said mournfully.

"Darrell made her go in today," Trina explained. "He said he wasn't going to listen to any more of her silly excuses."

"And he made her be partners with a boy!" Megan told her. "Erin didn't go in. I think she's got her period. So I was partners with Trina."

"Was it awful?" Katie asked.

Sarah shrugged. "Not too awful. Actually, he tried to be nice and show me some stuff. Of course, I didn't speak to him," she added hastily. "Is that okay? I mean, did I break our vow?"

"I guess not," Katie said uneasily. "I mean, if Darrell forced you, there's nothing you can do about it. You don't want to be reported to Ms. Winkle."

Sarah sighed in relief. "That's good. I don't want to end up like Erin."

Katie smiled thinly. "Yeah. Same here."

Chapter 6

"You want to go riding?" Trina asked Katie that afternoon.

"I can't," Katie replied. "The stirrups would rub against my rash. I guess I'll just go over to the arts and crafts cabin and work on the dollhouse."

"Is that fun?" Sarah asked. "Maybe I should work on that with you."

Katie's heartbeat quickened, and she thought frantically. "It's no fun at all. Actually, it's kind of boring. I'm only going to work on it to take my mind off the itching."

"Oh." Sarah flopped down on her bed. "In that case, I'll finish my book."

Katie allowed herself a small sigh of relief. It was too bad she had to discourage Sarah, though. If they were going to get that dollhouse finished for the hospital, they could use all the help they could get.

The arts and crafts cabin was empty when she

got there. Katie went to the back of the room and examined the dollhouse. There were a lot of rooms to fill. She didn't even know where to begin. She really needed Justin's help. But we'll just work, she promised herself. I won't talk to him, anymore than I absolutely have to.

A few seconds later, Justin appeared. He gave Katie a lopsided grin. "Hi."

"Hi," Katie replied.

"How does your ankle feel?"

"It itches a little, but it's not too bad. How's your arm?"

Justin shrugged. "It's okay." He reached into his pocket and pulled out a white glove. "The doctor gave me this to put on my hand, so I can work on the furniture." He put the glove on and held up his hand. "How's this? Do I look like Michael Jackson?"

Despite herself, Katie grinned. "Exactly. Now, let's see you sing and dance."

"I'm better at making furniture," Justin replied. "You know, we could use this Styrofoam to make kitchen stuff, like a stove and a refrigerator."

They got to work. Justin showed her how to cut the soft white Styrofoam so it wouldn't shred. Katie tried to pay attention, but she kept glancing nervously at the door.

"Look," she said to Justin, "if anyone comes in, we can't speak to each other, okay?"

"I know, I know, you said that before."

"Well, I just wanted to remind you."

"I don't need reminding," Justin retorted. "I'm not a moron, you know. Now quit looking at the door. You have to pay attention if you want to learn how to do this."

Katie eyed him haughtily. "I *am* paying attention." What a know-it-all, she thought. Typical boy. She better impress him right away before he decided that *she* was a moron.

"I think it would be nice to give this house a name," she stated.

Justin's forehead wrinkled. "A name? What for?"

"Because it would look elegant," Katie told him. "In England, lots of houses have names."

"This isn't England," Justin stated.

"So what? Besides, some houses here have names too. I have a friend whose parents have a house on the beach. It's named Seascape. It's on a sign above the door."

"Well, I think it's a dumb idea."

"You're just not mature enough to appreciate it," Katie snapped.

Justin groaned. "Okay, we'll give the house a name. What do you want to call it?"

This was what Katie had been waiting for. She pretended to think for minute. "How about Serendipity?"

"Serendipity?"

"Yes." This was a chance to show off her vocabulary. "It means something nice that happens by accident."

"I know what it means," Justin said.

Sure you do, Katie thought. "Can you spell it?"

"Sure," Justin replied. "S-E-R-E-N-D-I-P-I-T-Y."

Katie was surprised. "That's right!"

"Of course it's right," Justin said matter-of-factly. "I won a spelling bee on that word."

"What kind of spelling bee?"

"Last year, in my school."

"You're kidding!" Katie exclaimed. "I won the spelling bee at my school last year too. Were you in the district contest too?"

"Yeah." This time Justin didn't look quite so proud. "I only came in third."

Now Katie was astonished. "Really? I came in third in *my* district."

Justin's eyebrows shot up. "That's a real coincidence." Then he grinned. "C-O-I-N-C-I-D-E-N-C-E."

Katie nodded. "Positively phenomenal. P-H-E-N-O-M-E-N-A-L." And then she giggled. Justin's grin widened.

"It looks like we've got something in common. What's your favorite subject at school?"

"Language arts," Katie said promptly. "Especially reading. What's yours?"

"Same thing. Social studies is my second favorite."

"Mine too. What's your worst?"

Justin made a face. "Math. And I'm not too crazy about science."

"Me neither."

Justin stared at her. "This is amazing." Then he held up the little white Styrofoam cube. "How can we make this look more like a stove?"

Katie examined it. "We could cut round discs out of construction paper and paste them on top for burners. No, wait, I've got a better idea." She went over to the storage cabinet. After searching for a minute, she returned triumphantly with a box of paper clips.

"Look!" She pulled out a circular silver-colored clip. "We could use these."

"Great!" Justin exclaimed. "And we could color them black with a marker!"

Katie poked around in the box of clips until she found three more of the circular kind. And she found something else too—pins, with round black heads. "We could use these for knobs!"

They got to work. Within minutes, they were gazing proudly at what looked like an actual miniature stove.

"It's an absolute masterpiece," Justin declared. And then, as if they were reading each other's minds, they both chanted in unison, "M-A-S-T-E-R-P-I-E-C-E."

They were laughing so hard, neither of them heard the door open. Katie practically jumped when she heard a voice say, "Hi, kids."

She whirled around in a panic. Luckily, it was

only Donna, the arts and crafts counselor. Katie was about to breath a sigh of relief, when she saw that Donna wasn't alone. Behind her was Carolyn.

Justin didn't notice the panic on Katie's face. "Look at this," he said to Donna, holding up the stove. Donna examined it.

"This is terrific! I'm glad you guys decided to work together after all."

Katie hoped her voice wasn't trembling. "It's not because we want to," she said coldly. "It's just because we have to get it finished for the kids in the hospital. I'd much rather be doing this by myself."

Out of the corner of her eye, she could tell that Justin was looking at her. And from his expression, she had the sinking feeling that she'd hurt his feelings. He'll just have to understand, she thought. She couldn't let Carolyn know they were actually getting along. What if she told the other girls?

Carolyn was looking at her watch. "I'd better get back to cabin six. It's almost time for dinner. You coming, Katie?"

"Yeah." Katie took the paper clip box back to the cabinet. When she passed Justin, she wanted to tell him she didn't really mean what she had said. But Carolyn was watching them.

She didn't even say good-bye. And as soon as she got outside, she turned to Carolyn urgently.

"Listen, Carolyn, don't tell the others I was working with that boy, okay?"

"Oh, Katie, don't you think that's silly? Why don't you want them to know?"

"Because . . . because they might think I'm becoming friends with him. Which I'm not, of course," she added hastily. "And then I'd be breaking our vow. Like Erin."

"You're still not speaking to Erin?"

Katie nodded. "That's what we do to traitors. See, I was only working with Justin because . . . because I couldn't get him to leave. I wasn't talking to him. So I'm not a traitor like Erin. She's hanging around with a boy on purpose."

"But how do you think Erin feels about the way you girls are treating her?"

"If it bothers her, she should stop seeing that boy. Then we'd all talk to her again."

She didn't expect Carolyn to really understand. And from Carolyn's face, she could tell the counselor didn't. But that wasn't important. What was important was to make sure Carolyn didn't say anything.

"You won't tell the others, will you? Please?"

Carolyn sighed. "There's no reason for me to tell anyone, Katie. But I do think you're all being silly."

Katie wasn't even listening to that last part. "Thanks," she said gratefully. Carolyn might be just another dippy counselor, but Katie had a pretty good feeling she could be trusted.

She still didn't feel great about this. A fleeting image of Justin's hurt expression crossed her mind. But she could make him understand. And maybe they could meet again tomorrow.

Chapter 7

"Where's Erin?" Carolyn asked the girls when she joined them for lunch the next day.

"She's over there," Trina told her, indicating a table on the other side of the room. Erin was eating with some cabin nine girls. A couple of the older boys were sitting with them.

Carolyn eyed the cabin six girls reproachfully. "Are you girls still giving her the silent treatment?" She seemed to be looking at Katie pointedly. Katie swallowed. So far Carolyn had kept her word. But she'd better try to stay on her good side.

"She *wants* to sit with those kids," Katie declared. She didn't mention the fact that Erin had sat down at the cabin six table first. But after a few minutes, she'd realized that no one was speaking to her, and she'd picked up her tray and left.

Carolyn still had that look of disapproval on her face, so Katie figured she'd better change the subject before they got a lecture. "Sarah, did Darrell make you go in the water again this morning?"

Sarah nodded. "He says I have to learn to kick and stroke at the same time. That's even harder than patting your head and rubbing your stomach."

"Did you have to swim with that boy again?" Katie asked her.

"Yeah."

"That's terrible," Katie said. "It must be awful having to be partners with someone you can't even speak to. Darrell shouldn't make you do that."

Sarah didn't say anything. She seemed terribly interested in her macaroni and cheese. And Katie felt guilty. It was bad enough that Sarah had to go in the water, not to mention the fact that she couldn't even talk to her partner. Sarah would never break a cabin vow.

But Katie had. And she felt sick about it inside. "You won't have to swim with him for much longer," she told Sarah. "I'll be able to go back in the water in a couple of days. Then you and I can be partners."

Sarah nodded, but she didn't look at her. Suddenly, Katie felt a little uneasy. Did Sarah know something? Had she looked in the arts and crafts cabin this morning after swimming and seen Katie with Justin?

"I can't wait till I can go swimming again," she announced. "This morning I had absolutely nothing to do. So I ended up just walking around, doing nothing."

Megan looked up. "You weren't down by the tennis courts, were you?"

"No. Why?"

"Oh, I was just wondering." She jumped up. "I'm going for seconds."

Katie's eyes followed her. Everyone seemed so out-of-it today. It must be the boys, she thought. They were getting on everyone's nerves.

"There's a trip into Pine Ridge this afternoon," Carolyn announced. "Anyone want to go?"

"I'll go," Trina said. "Katie, are you coming?"

Katie quickly crammed a forkful of macaroni in her mouth, to give herself time to think. She'd sort of planned to work on the dollhouse that afternoon. But if she didn't start hanging out more with the girls, they might get suspicious.

She swallowed. "Yeah, I'm going. Sarah, you want to go to Pine Ridge?" Going into the village was one of Sarah's favorite camp activities. She could spend the whole afternoon in the bookstore.

To her surprise, Sarah shook her head. "No, there's, uh, something I want to do." And then she got up. "I'm going back for seconds."

Megan returned to the table. "Are you coming to Pine Ridge?" Katie asked her.

"No," Megan replied. "I want to play tennis this afternoon."

"Did you find someone to play with?" Trina asked.

"Not exactly," Megan said. "But I saw someone playing yesterday who looked pretty good."

"One of the older girls?" Katie asked. But Megan had her mouth full and didn't answer. Katie gave an exaggerated sigh. "I hope none of the *boys* are going to Pine Ridge."

"Speaking of boys," Megan said, "there goes your buddy, Katie."

Katie glanced up, and saw Justin passing. For a second, their eyes met. Then, they both immediately looked away.

"What do you mean, my *buddy?*" she asked Megan. "You know I can't stand him!"

Megan blinked. "I was just making a joke!"

Katie pushed her tray aside. "I'm going back to the cabin. What time does the bus leave?"

"Right after rest period," Carolyn told her. "You're supposed to meet in front of arts and crafts." She got up to return her tray. As soon as she was out of earshot, Katie whispered in Trina's ear. "I'm going to sneak into arts and crafts during rest period. Put pillows under my sheet so it looks like I'm napping, in case Carolyn checks on us, okay?"

Trina looked surprised, but she nodded. Katie returned her tray, and hurried over to the arts and crafts cabin. Justin was already there.

"Did anyone see you come in here?" she asked him. Justin shook his head. He was sanding down the little table they'd made that morning.

"This looks good," he said. "Let's start on the chairs."

Katie agreed, and they got to work. For a few minutes, they worked in silence. "You know," Justin said suddenly, "it's really stupid that we have to sneak around like this to meet."

"I know," Katie said. "This rest period business is really dumb. They treat us like we're still babies who need a nap."

"That's not what I mean. I'm talking about how we can't let anyone know we're working together. That's even dumber than the rest period."

"It's just the way it is," Katie said lamely. That morning, she'd promised herself they'd just work and not talk. That way, it didn't seem so much like she was breaking the cabin vow. But it wasn't easy being alone with someone and not speaking at all.

"I had an idea," Justin said. He reached into his pocket and pulled out a postcard. "Look at this stamp."

The stamp was a picture of some flowers, and the cancellation mark had barely touched it. "It's pretty," Katie said. "Do you collect stamps?"

"Yeah. Do you?"

Katie nodded. This was incredible. How could she have this much in common with a boy?

"I was thinking," Justin said, "we could make a tiny frame for this stamp, and hang it in the dollhouse as a painting."

"Neat!" Katie exclaimed. She searched through

the materials lying on the table. "We could use these little strips of balsa wood." Carefully, she began cutting strips of wood to fit the stamp. "Justin . . ."

"Huh?"

"Did you really make dollhouse furniture for your kid sister, like you told Donna?"

"Yeah. Why?"

Katie sighed. "My brothers never do anything nice for me."

Justin looked at her quizzically. "Never?"

Katie was about to repeat "never," but then she remembered something—that pretty little box they'd given her before she left. Then there was the time she fell and cut her knee roller skating, and her parents weren't home, and Peter took her to the emergency room. He was pretty nice that day. And she remembered the time she got in trouble for something, and she was sent to her room without dessert. Michael sneaked her some pudding.

"Almost never," she said. "I mean, we fight a lot."

Justin grinned. "My sister and I fight a lot too. I think that's what brothers and sisters are supposed to do."

Just then, Katie heard some noise outside. She went over to the window and peered out. "Oh, no! The buses are here to take us to Pine Ridge! What if someone sees us together?"

"I'm not going to Pine Ridge," Justin told her. "I'm supposed to meet some guys at the pool."

Kids were gathering outside, and getting on the two vans. Katie could see Trina there, looking around. What if she looked inside the cabin? She thought quickly. "Would you mind getting under the table until the vans leave? I can't let Trina find out I've been with you."

Justin rolled his eyes.

"There are *boys* out there," Katie pressed. "You don't want them to see you with me either!"

Justin groaned, but he nodded. "Yeah, okay." He got under the table. As Katie hurried toward the door, she could hear him mumbling, "This is getting ridiculous." She had to admit he was right. But there was nothing they could do about it now.

"There you are," Trina said when Katie came up to her. "I was just about to go in the cabin and get you."

That was a close call, Katie thought. She'd better start being more careful. "Let's go," she said, and started toward a van. Trina stopped her. "There are boys on that one."

Katie wrinkled her nose. "Yuck!" She put an extra note of disgust in her voice to impress Trina. They ran over to the other bus and got on.

The ride was only twenty minutes. Since they were upper campers, Katie and Trina were allowed to go off on their own as long as they stayed on the village Main Street. "Meet back here in front of the drug store in one hour," the counselor instructed them as she led the younger campers away.

"What do you want to do first?" Katie asked Trina.

"Sarah gave me money to get a book for her," Trina said. They headed down the road to the bookstore. "Do you know what the movie's going to be tonight?"

Katie had forgotten this was movie-by-the-lake night. "No. I hope it's not cartoons." She paused. "I'll bet Erin sits with that boy she went canoeing with and pretends she's having a date." She made a gagging sound.

Trina was silent for a moment. "I feel sort of bad about the way we're treating Erin."

"It's her own fault," Katie pointed out. "Anyway, she doesn't care that we're not speaking to her."

"I think she *does* care," Trina said. "She just acts like she doesn't."

Katie shrugged. "Well, she puts on a good act. I couldn't do that. If everyone stopped speaking to me, I'd be really upset." Just the thought of it made her shudder.

"Me, too," Trina agreed fervently.

The little bookstore was practically empty. The girls headed directly toward the back, where the young adult paperback books were shelved. "What book does Sarah want?" Katie asked.

"She wants a mystery."

Katie scanned the shelves, and picked out a book. "Do you think this looks good?"

But Trina was busy looking at something else. "Isn't that one of the boys at Sunnyside?" she asked in a whisper.

Katie turned to see. The boy standing a few yards away did look familiar. She made a face. "We just can't get away from them. I didn't think we'd see any of them in here. Boys don't read."

But this boy seemed intent on finding something to read. He was examining the titles on the shelves, and frowning. Trina and Katie watched him.

"I guess he can't find what he's looking for," Trina said softly.

Katie smirked. "Probably comic books."

A saleslady approached the boy. "Can I help you find something?"

The boy's face went a little pink, but he nodded. He mumbled something to the lady. Katie couldn't hear him.

"A book about divorce?" the saleslady asked loudly. Now the boy's face was practically crimson. "Now, let me see. We did have a book for young people, *How to Cope When Your Parents Divorce*." She ran her eyes across the shelf. "We seem to be out of it, though. Would you like me to order it for you?"

Just then, the boy noticed Katie and Trina watching him. "Never mind," he mumbled, and hurried out of the store.

102

Katie looked at Trina. Her friend's eyes were sad. "I know how he feels," she said. "When my parents split up, I ran around looking for books about it."

"Did you find any?"

"Two. And they were pretty good. I even brought one of them to camp. Sometimes, when I feel depressed about my parents, I read parts of it and it makes me feel better."

Katie nodded understandingly. She had books that made her feel better when she was sad, too. She hoped all the fuss over the boys was enough to take Trina's mind off her parents.

The girls bought the book for Sarah, and went outside. "There's that boy," Katie remarked. He was looking in the window of a small grocery store. "You want to go look at records?"

"All right," Trina said. They crossed the street and headed to the record store. But just as they reached it, Trina stopped and clapped a hand to her mouth. "I just remembered something. I promised Megan I'd get her some chocolate chip cookies. I'll go get them now, and meet you back here."

"Okay." Katie went on into the record store. As she wandered over to the rock section, she saw a couple of the boys from camp. Flipping through a stack of records, she glanced occasionally at them. And she found herself wondering if they were okay, like Justin. She strained to hear what they were saying.

"I've got this Michael Jackson album," one of them said to the other.

"Me too. I like it better than the last one."

Katie could see the album they were talking about. She had it too. She wondered which song they liked best. She wanted to ask them, but decided against it. Trina could walk in any minute.

And she did. "Hi," she said breathlessly. She looked a little flushed. "Are you going to buy that?"

Katie put back the album she was holding. "No, I was just looking at it. Where are the cookies?"

"What cookies?"

"The cookies you went to buy for Megan."

Trina stared at her for a minute. "Oh! Yeah, well, they didn't have any. Um, you want to go get some ice cream?"

"Okay," Katie said. But she looked at Trina curiously. No chocolate chip cookies in a grocery store? She'd never heard of such a thing.

No one was in the cabin when they got back. Trina went into the bathroom to take a shower, and Katie was debating a quick trip to arts and crafts before dinner when Megan burst in, swinging her tennis racket.

"Boy, that was a great game!" she crowed. "And I won!"

"Who'd you play with?" Katie asked.

"Oh, this kid I met . . . what did you guys do in Pine Ridge?"

"Not much. Oh, Trina couldn't find the cookies you wanted."

Megan looked at her in confusion. "What cookies?"

"Didn't you ask Trina to get you some chocolate chip cookies?"

"I don't *think* so," Megan said slowly. "Maybe I did and I forgot." She looked out the window. "Here comes Sarah. Wow, I can't believe it! She looks like she's been swimming!"

"During free time?" Katie couldn't believe it either. Sarah would never go swimming on her own free will. But sure enough, she was wearing a bathing suit, and her hair was wet. And she was *smiling*.

"I did it!" she declared happily. "I kicked and stroked at the same time! For at least two minutes before I sank!"

"Did Darrell help you?" Megan asked. She did a little swoon. "Lucky you. Sometimes I want to pretend I don't know how to swim just so I can get Darrell to help me."

Before Sarah could answer, the cabin door opened and Erin walked in. Everyone fell silent.

Erin stared at them stonily. "Don't worry, I'm not hanging around. I just came back to take a shower before dinner. If that's okay with you." She went over to the dresser by her bed and pulled out a toiletry kit. When she passed by, Katie could see that her lips were set in a thin, angry line. She could also see that Erin's eyes were wet.

Even after she went into the shower, no one spoke. Looking around, Katie could tell that everyone felt uncomfortable. But no one could be feeling as bad about this as she did right that minute. Because she knew she was just as guilty of breaking their vow as Erin was.

Chapter 8

The girls were getting ready to leave for the movie that evening when Carolyn came into the cabin. "Well, I have some news that I'm sure will make you girls happy. The repairs are almost finished at Camp Eagle, and the boys will be leaving on Tuesday."

Katie gasped. That was only two days away! There was no way she and Justin could finish furnishing the dollhouse by then.

She realized that Carolyn was looking at her strangely. "I thought I'd be hearing cheers from you guys."

They're probably waiting to hear my reaction, Katie thought. "That's good news," she said quickly. "But it still means two more days with boys. If you told me they were leaving right this minute, I'd be cheering."

"I think you can manage for two more days," Carolyn said sternly. Then her expression softened. "Look, guys, I'm not going to lecture you on

107

the way you've been treating the boys. I guess when I was your age, I felt pretty much the same way about them. I just wish you wouldn't ostracize Erin. Where is Erin, anyway?''

"Probably down by the lake already," Megan said.

"Sitting with a *boy,*" Katie added for effect.

"Well, I'm going down there to help set up the movie," Carolyn said. "I'll see you there."

"What does 'ostracize' mean," Megan asked after she left.

"It means to exclude someone," Sarah replied.

"Oh. I thought it had something to do with putting your head in the sand. Like an ostrich. Ha-ha."

No one laughed. Katie was thinking about Justin. They absolutely had to find more time to work on the dollhouse—and still not let anyone see them doing it. She decided she'd try to talk to him tonight, during the movie, in the dark when no one was looking.

It dawned on her that the room was unusually quiet, as if everyone was thinking about something. Probably Erin, Katie thought. And once again she felt those guilty pangs. "Listen, you guys," she said slowly. "I was thinking . . . maybe we should make up with Erin. I mean, she broke her vow, and that's really terrible, but . . ."

"You're right," Trina said quickly. "I think we should talk to her *tonight.*"

"And maybe even apologize for the way we've been treating her," Sarah suggested.

Katie gazed at them curiously. They were being awfully quick to forgive and forget. That was not typical cabin six behavior.

"Let's go," Megan declared. "It's almost time for the movie."

"Sarah, don't forget your glasses," Trina said.

"I'm not going."

Everyone turned to her in surprise. "Why not?" Katie asked.

Sarah held up a book. "It's this mystery you brought me back from Pine Ridge. I'm right in the middle of it and I can't put it down."

"Oh, c'mon," Katie urged. "You can read it anytime. And we don't get a movie every night."

Sarah shook her head firmly. "I feel like reading." And as if to demonstrate this, she lay back on her bed and buried her face in the book.

"I wonder if something's wrong with her," Katie mused as she walked with Trina and Megan down to the lake. "Why is she being so stubborn all of a sudden?"

Neither Trina nor Megan replied. They both seemed caught up in their own thoughts. Then Katie noticed something. "Trina, why are you bringing a book with you?"

"In case the movie's boring," Trina said.

"But it'll be too dark. How are you going to read it?"

"Look!" Megan said. "There's Erin. Should we go talk to her now?"

But Katie had spotted someone else in the crowd of campers sprawled along the lakefront. "Um, let's wait till after the movie. I'll go get us some popcorn."

She left Megan and Trina settling down on the ground, and headed toward the table where sacks of popcorn and sodas were lying. Then, when she was sure the girls couldn't see her, she veered away from the refreshments.

Justin was sitting with a group of boys. Katie stared fixedly at him, until she finally caught his eye. Then she beckoned. Luckily, the other boys didn't see her.

"I'm going to get some more popcorn," she heard Justin announce to his friends. Then he got up and hurried over toward her.

"I just found out we're going back to Eagle on Tuesday," he told her, glancing back over his shoulder to make sure none of the boys were watching him.

"I know! And we've still got a lot of work to do on the dollhouse. You want to work on it tonight?"

"While the movie's going on?"

Katie nodded. "Everyone will be down here so we'll be safe. Let's wait till the movie gets started, and then we can sneak away."

Justin agreed. "Okay. I'll meet you at the arts

and crafts cabin fifteen minutes after the movie starts."

Katie picked up some popcorn and ran back to Megan and Trina.

The movie was starting and the credits were rolling when Trina turned to Katie. "I've already seen this," she whispered. "I'm going back to the cabin." And she got up and ran off.

"Why is she so jumpy?" Katie asked Megan. But Megan wasn't listening. She wasn't looking at the screen either. Her eyes seemed to be searching the crowd.

Katie squinted at her watch. She couldn't make out the dial in the dark. She stared at the screen for a few minutes.

"I'm going to get a soda," she whispered to Megan. But Megan wasn't there. Katie figured she must have gone to get some more refreshments. Quietly, Katie crept away, moving through the crowd. Then she scrambled up the banks and hurried toward the arts and crafts cabin.

She's almost made it to the door when she heard footsteps running behind her. She turned, expecting to see Justin.

"Erin! What are you doing here?"

Erin faced her squarely, her hands on her hips. "I want to talk to you."

Katie looked around nervously. Justin could be there any minute. "Can't we talk later?"

"No! I want to tell you that I think the vow we took was really stupid, and I think you guys have been really rotten to me. And I can't stand it anymore! Do you know what it feels like, when no one will speak to you?"

It couldn't feel any worse than the way Katie was feeling right that minute.

"So I told Bobby I won't see him anymore. Now are you satisfied?"

Katie didn't know what to say. Then the door to the cabin opened, and Justin stuck his head out. "C'mon, Katie, let's get to work." Then he realized Katie wasn't alone. "Uh-oh."

Katie waited for the ground to open up and swallow her. When it didn't, she raised her eyes slowly to meet Erin's furious face. "Why, you little sneak! You've been talking to boys too!"

"Shh," Justin said suddenly. "Someone's coming!" He ducked back into the cabin. Katie flattened herself against the wall. Now she could hear voices.

"I was really depressed when my Mom told me about the divorce. I was afraid maybe it was my fault."

It was Trina! And Katie was even more taken aback when she heard the other voice. "Yeah, that's how I was feeling too." It was a boy! And when they came into view, Katie recognized him. It was the boy they'd seen in the bookshop in Pine Ridge.

When Trina saw Katie and Erin, she froze. "Oh, no," she whispered.

"I can't believe this!" Erin exclaimed angrily.

"Both of you were treating me like I was some sort of traitor! And here you were both doing the same thing!"

Trina turned wide eyes to Katie. "Both?"

Katie gave up. "Let's go inside," she said meekly.

Justin seemed just as stunned to see Trina and the boy as Katie was. "Larry! What are you doing here?"

Larry looked abashed. "I met Trina in Pine Ridge. She said she had this book on divorce she'd lend me."

So that's why Trina pretended to look for chocolate chip cookies, Katie realized. She was talking to this Larry!

"What are *you* doing here?" Larry asked Justin.

"Katie and I have been working on this dollhouse furniture."

"You mean, you've been sneaking around meeting him?" Trina asked her reproachfully. "And I was so afraid you'd find out I've been talking to Larry."

Katie could barely meet her eyes. "Yeah. I guess Sarah and Megan are the only ones keeping the vow."

"I hear footsteps," Larry said suddenly. "It might be a counselor! Turn off the lights!" Justin hit the switch, and they all dived under tables.

The cabin door opened. "I'm pretty sure I left my racket in here this afternoon," a boy's voice declared. The lights went on. And Katie couldn't believe it when she saw who was with the boy.

"Megan!"

Megan bent down and peered under the table. "Katie?"

Slowly, Katie crawled out. Erin, Trina, Larry, and Justin followed. And they all stood there in silence, with the same sheepish expression. Except for Erin. *She* looked triumphant.

"You've *all* been seeing boys. Except for Sarah."

"I needed someone to play tennis with," Megan said plaintively. "Stewart's the best player here."

Katie offered her a thin smile. "I guess you don't have to make any excuses. Like Erin said, we're all guilty. Except Sarah."

Megan's mouth dropped open. "You mean, we've all been running around meeting boys in secret?"

And then it was as if they all realized at the very same moment how silly they'd been. Trina giggled first. Megan followed. And before long, they were all laughing like hyenas.

They made so much noise, they didn't hear the cabin door open again. "What's going on here!"

Carolyn stood there, her arms folded across her chest. And she didn't look at all happy to see them. "I couldn't find any of you at the movie. And when I went back to the cabin, no one was there either! Do you have any idea how worried I've been?"

"Wait a minute," Trina said. "Wasn't Sarah in the cabin?"

"No. Isn't she with you?"

The girls shook her head. Then Trina gasped. "She's been so excited about learning to swim. You don't think—"

"She's down at the pool by herself?" Katie asked. "But Sarah can barely swim at all!"

Now Carolyn looked frightened. "Come with me," she ordered. And the whole group hurried out of the cabin and started running toward the pool.

Someone was swimming. They could hear splashing as they approached in the darkness. And there were voices too.

"Great! Now, keep your hands together and try it again."

By the light of the moon, Katie saw a boy sitting on the edge of the pool. He was carefully watching someone under the water. And then that someone emerged, beaming happily—until she saw the group gathered on the side.

"Uh-oh."

"Sarah!" Erin practically shrieked. "Not you too!"

Sarah pushed her hair out of her eyes. She gazed at the boys and girls in confusion. Then her expression changed, and it was clear that she'd figured out what was going on. And she grinned sheepishly.

"Yeah. Me too."

Chapter 9

Back in their cabin, the girls huddled on their beds, waiting for the lecture they knew was coming. Carolyn's expression was stern, but at least she didn't look as furious as she had at the pool. And Katie could have sworn there was the tiniest glint of humor in her eyes.

"Now, would you all mind telling me what's been going on around here?"

Erin spoke first in an injured tone. "They said I was a traitor for breaking the vow and talking to a boy. And they were doing the same thing! It was a conspiracy!"

"It was not," Katie argued. "I thought I was the only one. Justin and I were working on dollhouse furniture. And that's the only reason I had anything to do with him."

"Hah!" Erin retorted. "I saw the way he looked at you. You guys are *friends.*"

Katie couldn't exactly call her a liar. "Well . . . maybe. Just a little."

116

Megan went next. "I couldn't find anyone to play tennis with me. And then I saw Stewart playing." She sighed. "He was great. We pretended he was Boris Becker and I was Steffi Graf and we were at Wimbledon."

"And what about you, Sarah?" Carolyn asked. "You could have drowned in that pool!"

"Oh no," Sarah replied solemnly. "Patrick's an excellent swimmer." She hugged the towel wrapped around her. "When Darrell made me be partners with him, I promised everyone I wouldn't talk to him. But he was so nice! And he offered to help me practice. I didn't mean to break our vow, but I *had* to speak to him."

Erin turned to Trina. "Who was the boy you were with? He was kind of cute."

Trina replied with dignity. "That's not why I was seeing him. His parents are getting divorced, and he needed to talk to someone who understands what that feels like. I didn't want to break our vow either, but I felt so sorry for him."

Carolyn put her hands to her head as if she was about to tear her hair out. "I'm sick of hearing about breaking that stupid vow! You should be more worried about the way you treated Erin. That's not the way friends are supposed to act."

The girls exchanged glances. "We're sorry," Katie said meekly.

"I'm not the one you should be apologizing to," Carolyn said.

They all turned to Erin, who looked at them

117

smugly. "Sorry, Erin," Katie murmured, and the others echoed this.

"I accept your apology," Erin replied graciously. "But you all better be really nice to me for the rest of the summer."

Katie couldn't help smiling. Erin was loving this! Then she thought of something that made her smile fade. "It's too bad they're leaving on Tuesday. There's no way Justin and I can get that dollhouse finished."

"And I won't have anyone to play tennis with," Megan added mournfully.

"That's not necessarily true," Carolyn told them. "Ms. Winkle's been talking to the director at Camp Eagle. They're thinking about arranging activities the two camps can do together, and letting campers visit."

Katie brightened. "You mean, Justin might be able to come here for arts and crafts?"

"It's a possibility," Carolyn replied. "Of course, she might very well change her mind if she knew how you kids have been behaving."

"Are you going to tell her?" Megan asked anxiously.

Carolyn paused and studied their faces. "I won't tell, on one condition. If you promise not to do anything so stupid again this summer. Okay?"

The girls looked at each other again. "How can we tell if what we're planning on doing is stupid or not?" Katie asked.

Carolyn through up her hands. "Forget it! Look,

just tell me this. Have you *learned* anything from this experience?"

Trina spoke hesitantly. "I *think* so. I've learned that some boys can be nice."

Katie nodded. "Yeah, it's kind of a miracle, isn't it? With all the creepy boys in the world, we managed to find five halfway decent ones."

Carolyn smiled at her. "I can assure you, Katie, there are quite a few more. And I have a feeling, that as you get older, you're going to find them."

Katie made a face. She hated when grown-ups said things like that. Okay, maybe not all boys were obnoxious. And maybe there were a few others, like Justin, who were interesting and smart and nice.

But could they make decent dollhouse furniture? She doubted it.